Reviews of *The Swill*

"*The Swill* takes the reader on a winding and unpredictable path through history and class where every surface sparkles brilliantly with period detail. Gutierrez twines a half century of skullduggery, of Pinkertons, gangsters, speakeasies, of family, family secrets, and betrayals, into an arresting tale that is brutal, tender, and riveting. He writes unsentimentally, with humor, and with a deep and abiding love for the novel's real subject, which is that of history and how deeply and intimately it connects us and shapes our fates. That is Gutierrez's real genius and what makes this thriller so much more, what makes it so memorable."

– **Alexander Parsons**, director of creative writing at the University of Houston and author of *In the Shadows of the Sun*

"Atmospheric and taut, Michael Gutierrez's *The Swill* is an enthralling, raucous novel about art and history and violence. Imagine a barroom, low lit and pulsing with story, and imagine that story being told by Hemingway, Tarantino and Denis Johnson. That is Michael Gutierrez and his fabulous novel, *The Swill*."

– **Travis Mulhauser**, author of *Sweet Girl*

Reviews for *The Trench Angel*

"An inherently absorbing and exceptionally well crafted novel from beginning to end, *The Trench Angel* showcases the extraordinary storytelling talents of author Michael Keenan Gutierrez. *The Trench Angel* is very highly recommended for community library Mystery/Suspense collections."
– *Midwest Book Review*

"Gutierrez's debut sets the industrialized murder of World War I as backdrop to the murderous industry of coal mining in the American West circa 1919.... While Gutierrez draws Paris, the Belgian warfront, and the rough-hewn frontier town with a good eye —"the sun hovered over the Rocky peaks, shading the mountain snow like a bruise"— the novel's unfiltered lens reveals war's cost to the human psyche, the amorality of concentrated wealth, the cancer of racial and ethnic hatred, and the nearly unresolvable conflict between familial loyalty and moral responsibility. By turns lyrical and brutal, Gutierrez stretches an intriguing piece of historical fiction to cover multiple themes." – *Kirkus*

"*The Trench Angel* is a vivid and engaging novel and it carries a doomed, bloody and wondrous vision of the World War I trenches and the American West in the years after The Great War. It's also a ripping good yarn." – **John Dalton**, *Heaven Lake*

THE

SWILL

BY MICHAEL KEENAN GUTIERREZ

Also by the Author
The Trench Angel

THE
SWILL

BY MICHAEL KEENAN GUTIERREZ

Leapfrog Press
New York and London

Published in 2022 in the United States by
Leapfrog Press Inc.

www.leapfrogpress.com

Distributed in the United States by
Consortium Book Sales and Distribution
St. Paul, Minnesota 55114
www.cbsd.com

First Edition

ISBN 978-1-948585-39-2

Author photo: © Ronnie Glenn

Library of Congress Cataloging-in-Publication Data

Printed and bound in the United Kingdom

The Forest Stewardship Council® is an international
non-governmental organisation that promotes environmentally
appropriate, socially beneficial, and economically viable management
of the world's forests. To learn more visit www.fsc.org

TABLE OF CONTENTS

To my mother

It avails not, time nor place – distance avails not,
I am with you, you men and women of a generation, or ever so
many generations hence,
Just as you feel when you look on the river and sky, so I felt,
Just as any of you is one of a living crowd, I was one of a crowd,
Just as you are refresh'd by the gladness of the river and the
bright flow, I was refresh'd
Just as you stand and lean on the rail, yet hurry with the swift
current, I stood yet was hurried,
Just as you look on the numberless masts of ships and the thick-
stemm'd pipes of Steamboats, I look'd.

—Walt Whitman

PART ONE: DEBTS

CHAPTER ONE

March 13, 1929—Port Kydd, USA

Ice spackled the basement panes, high up, out of reach. The old glass shivered but held. Elms froze and groaned. Sirens flared. And below the street, down in the old tavern, Joshua Rivers had just rung the bell for last call when his sister blew through the door.

He hadn't seen her in almost a year, so when she came down with unsteady steps, like she hadn't been born upstairs, he almost didn't recognize her. She was dressed in the fashion of the day—a cloche hat and satin blue dress cut just at the knees—but the way she wore it felt like a disguise. Her hair was pinned under the hat and her posture was sunken. Confidence got eyes following you across the floor, and the way she held herself told him that she wanted to disappear into the crowd.

She slipped past the long table, two-stepping between a handful from the neighborhood, old men and women nursing their beers, stretching a dime until the end of the evening. At the piano she tapped a couple of keys like she was making sure it had been kept in tune. It hadn't. From there she pivoted toward the bookshelves, taking down a paperback, skimming a

Chapter One

few pages, and then walking past him without so much as a nod, before settling against the bar, her shoulders slackening, a sigh audible from across the room.

He knew her game, so he went about ragging tables and emptying ashtrays, only pausing when a hand stopped on his hip and squeezed. The grabber was Marjorie O'Neil, an old bookkeeper who worked for a numbers runner over in Pinebox Square and had been coming to the Swill since before Prohibition. She drank straight rum most nights and when he was out she drank straight whiskey and when that was short, she took whatever he had behind the bar. Straight.

"Sit," she said.

He sat. His hands fell on his lap and he looked up at the splintering rafters, at the cobwebs, at the scratches and dents from raised fists and broken glasses, at the carvings of initials wrapped in hearts and skewered by arrows.

"We never talk," Marjorie said. "Wasn't there a time when we talked all the time? You had such a beautiful voice back then."

Across the room, his sister leaned over the bar, arm outstretched, coming up with a bottle of rail gin, no label. She poured a four-count into a highball glass. No one else seemed to notice.

"What happened to your voice?" Marjorie said. "So lovely. Like an opera singer or a Nancy-boy."

"You mean Rafael. My voice was never pretty."

"Maybe you're right. Does sound awful gravelly now. Like a mule bucked you in the throat. You look younger than you used to. What's your secret? Witchcraft?"

Joshua lit a cigarette and thanked her for the compliment. He'd take any he could get. He was a big man, six-five, but like a lot of big men, he'd developed a slouch to escape doorway knocks and scared looks. He was also red-headed and soft spoken, so that no one knew whether to find him threatening or simple. His face was babyish, nearly cherubic, and he only had to take a razor to it once a week. Still, he was 35, a war veteran, and no one was brave enough to tease him, at least in this neighborhood. They knew better. In the nicer parts of town, he looked like a red-headed ruffian, a guy you'd expect to find on "wanted" posters, but down in the Bonny his war exploits had made him famous, a local hero they could point to and say, "the Germans sure know they can't fuck with a boy from *our* neighborhood." He was also a business owner, a man with roots in the community and the Swill was at the center of it. Or it used to be. In the old days, it was where the ward boss met his constituents, where the Democratic machine planned its campaigns. On election day, people even came down there to vote. Joshua's grandmother had mediated truces between rival gangs, setting them up at the long table with pitchers of beer, and acting as umpire when words got sharp. But that had all moved to nicer speakeasies. Even though the Bonny saw the Swill as an institution as sacred as the church itself, legacy didn't settle debts.

"What were you saying?"

"You're having a baby," Marjorie said.

"No, my wife is."

"That's how it works, kiddo."

The chatter picked up like a crowd at intermission. Gabriel Rafferty, the local tanner, hands rubbed raw, eyes bloodshot, dropped three Jacks on Lucy Green, a dog trainer late of County Kerry. Lucy threw her cards across the room. "You no-good Scot bastard."

Joshua tensed. He knew Lucy to be quick with a razor, but when she fell onto Gabriel's lap for a kiss, he settled back down.

"If it is a boy you sire," Marjorie said. "You must be firm. Use the belt but not the buckle. Then they know you're tough but merciful. If you use the buckle, it's just out of meanness."

"No buckle. Got it."

"Boys can grow up hard here. Real mean. It's a pity. My Johnny was too sweet for this world. But the army was good for him. Made him a man."

And got him killed, Joshua thought.

"But if you have a girl, kiddo, you go talk to the penguins over at St. Nicholas about sizing her up for a coif and veil."

His sister reached for a neighboring pack of cigarettes, ones owned by Joanie Avery, who was napping on the next stool over. She struck a match against her boot, and brought the fire to her lips, before blowing a cloud up to the rafters the way their grandmother used to.

"If not the convent," Marjorie said, "then marry her as soon as she gets her woman's blood. Find a nice Danish boy. They don't beat their wives often and their wrists are so delicate it don't hurt none if they do."

"I'll think on it," Joshua said. "Though figuring she'll go and make her own way."

"Right to the whore's bed if you don't get smart, kiddo. Believe me."

"Glad we had this talk."

"You were so much nicer in the old days."

He excused himself to put up chairs so the leftovers would get the hint and head for the street. At the bar, his sister's gaze drifted above the kitchen door to a pair of old pistols, ones without firing pins, ones in need of a good cleaning that had been owned by his grandfather. There were a lot of things like that in the Swill, old junk that found its way onto the walls, turning the bar into a second-hand, cast-off museum of sorts. You had cracked frames showing off newspaper clippings of Lincoln's death, McKinley's death, alongside rusted shackles, a taxidermied Crabbe Rat, and a portrait of a Revolutionary whose name everyone had forgotten.

Chapter One

Soon, they all headed toward the stairs, none nearly drunk enough to sleep through dawn. It was midnight and some would return for lunch, and if not then, supper. The Swill was the sort of place you went every day or avoided altogether. Lately it had been more of the latter.

When the last customer shut the door, Joshua went to the bar and poured a whiskey. He raised his glass to his sister. "Cheers."

Her name was Olive Rivers, although she changed it whenever it suited her.

"Have you missed me?" she said.

She took off her hat, her blonde hair falling to her shoulders, starlet-like. She was pretty in the way Irish women were pretty before they got married and bore children and found that life was a series of church sermons, labor pains, and knock-down fights with unreliable husbands. Round face. Freckles. A resting smirk, like she'd pocketed cash from a nun's purse. A pair of lines ran along her forehead, the kind earned from squinting. He hadn't noticed them before. She'd just turned 30 and had been running cons since she was a teenager and he always worried that every time he saw her would be the last time.

"I did miss you," he said. "You can't go disappearing like that."

"I'm sorry."

"You don't sound sorry."

"Are you sure? I'm a very good liar."

"Olive."

"Look, a girl gets busy and forgets to write."

"I've heard you've been working."

"You have? What's the word?"

The word was that she'd knocked over a jewelry store up in the Jewish Quarter and played a stock scam on an heiress in Collier Park and that afterward she'd blown town without a goodbye. A few of the grimmer tales had her dead. All of these stories found their way into a small, wound ball in his gut where he jailed his fears. Even seeing her now made Joshua nervous. Tonight had felt like a fixed fight to begin with and he got the feeling that Olive had shown up to take a dive.

They stayed quiet for a moment, looking one another over, trying to get a sense of where each stood, only breaking their stare when Orla, a silver terrier, trotted over and Olive gave her a cold scratch under the chin.

"What happened to the old dog?" Olive asked. "Orla fifteen."

"This is Orla fifteen."

"Pretty sure this one is sixteen but what happened to *my* Orla?"

"Just got too old," he said.

"Feeling that." She took a long, cinematic breath and then smiled, playful. His sister was like that. She'd never taken anything too seriously, never wallowed in her own troubles or cared much for the sanctity of private property or the regard some held for the truth. It was all a big, dangerous joke. But even when she was playful, there was an underlying melancholy, one you saw when she closed her eyes to take a drink, that came across, at times, as fatalistic. It didn't bother him much, though. He shared that same melancholy. Like it was in the blood.

"You in trouble?" Joshua asked.

"No troubles. I'm swell. Now, you," she said, waving at the too-clean bar. "Cops even bother with their bribes?"

"We're getting by."

"How is my *lovely* sister-in-law?" Olive didn't like Lily.

"Pregnant. A few months, we think."

"I know. Congratulations."

"How?"

It was a stupid question and her look told him as much, as if he'd asked if Santa Claus was real. Even if she wasn't around, Olive knew *everything*, from the customers who'd been going

16

to other taverns, to how much he owed the milkman. It was as if she kept a crystal ball in the same bag as her lock picks and crowbar. At times, this sense she was always watching him from afar felt annoying. At other times, it felt like love.

"What are you going to name her?"

"Don't know yet," he said. "Lily thinks it's a boy."

"She's wrong."

Upstairs Lily padded from the bedroom down the stairs to the bathroom, while outside the Bonny was still coughing, ice storm or not. A dogfight down the street had just let out and some losers were skating their way back to their bone-chilling tenements. Down in the Swill, the electric lights flickered, and, out of habit, both looked toward the old gas jets, dormant since before the War. When the lights steadied, Olive went over to the old Revolutionary's portrait and ran her hand across the canvas, fingering the edge of his face, knocking cobwebs away from his wig.

"You still think this is Alexander Hamilton?" Olive asked.

"Sometimes. Sometimes James Madison or Sam Adams. You?"

"Eh, I think he's a nobody, a good for nothing foot soldier, probably a deserter, the sort who cheated at cards and skipped out on his tab. Makes sense, wouldn't it? Some families are bred as bankers because their daddies were bankers, and well, some were bred as—"

"Bank robbers?"

"Some got that trait, sure," she said. "No, this joker was no one you'd put on a nickel note. Probably just someone who bedded a barmaid and slipped out at dawn. It's the oldest story in town, our Garden of Eden tale."

She picked up the dog and cradled her. "You like art?"

"What?"

"Art," she said. "Paintings? Sculptures? Even a nice totem pole?"

Chapter One

He didn't. Couldn't even fake it, though he'd tried once because all of the smart people talked about it like they'd found Jesus. After the War, he'd done some work for the Pinkertons out in Chicago, guarding an art gallery near Lincoln Park, carrying a gun and a flashlight for a buck an hour. Along the walls hung Botticellis and Michelangelos gushed over by crowds in top hats and pearls. He stood off to the side and they looked past him like you would a horse hitched to a wagon. One night after locking up, he stopped in front of each painting, examining the images from far away and up close and all he felt was a numbness and wondered if his poverty had made him stupid.

"Nah," he said. "Prefer the picture show."

"You know they've got a talkie theater down on Graaf Street. Caught the Marx Brothers last week."

"The Marx Brothers, yeah," Joshua said. "I like the one who doesn't talk. He's funny."

She got up and started smelling the beer towels to see if they needed washing. Few did. He grabbed a broom.

"Why did you ask if I like art?"

"No reason." She was faced away from Joshua, so he couldn't see if she was lying. "I used to be a pretty good painter. Not as good as Grandma. She was good."

He took another drink, felt it finally hitting the right parts. Ever since Lily got pregnant, he'd been keeping to four drinks a day. Four seemed like a good number, a gentleman's number. Something a respectable father might uphold, but he got the feeling he was headed for six or seven tonight.

"Was wondering," she began, "if you were looking for some extra work?"

He stepped back and took a sip to think. It was cold down in the Swill, colder than it should have been because the coal man got paid late and they'd had to ration until the end of the month during the meanest winter he could remember, one that saw the Morgan River freeze clear across to Drakestown. The electric company sent bills on red paper and the butcher had threatened to skin him unless he paid up. It was all he could think about, the last of his pennies.

"Lily's pregnant. You heard me, right?"

"All the more reason to build up that nest egg." She paused a beat, putting up the last of the chairs. "Finishing school's expensive, I hear."

They laughed. He wiped his eyes.

"Don't tell me you've gone straight?"

He opened his hands to the bar.

"Running a speak isn't a real crime," she said.

"I'm doing fine."

"All right. All right. I get it."

After she finished her drink and headed for the door, he wanted to tell her to stay the night, to sleep in her old room, but it was a bad idea for Lily to see her in the morning.

"You change your mind," Olive said, "just give me a holler."

After locking the door, he returned to the register to count the night's take. He told himself that he wasn't worried as he wrapped his hand around a bottle. Upstairs, Lily slept, but she'd wake when he got into bed and ask how the night went and he couldn't bear to face her after another shift where they didn't break even. So he had another drink and sat at the piano to play an old song, a song no one played anymore, a song he played fine but without heart. He remembered how his sister played, fast and loose, as if she was making up her own melody as she went along. She was always more jazz that way, while he was baroque.

He shut his eyes, and when he couldn't shut off his thoughts, he grabbed his coat and his army revolver and headed into the ice storm.

It was past midnight and his fists were deep in his coat, ice crusting to his shoulders. He was used to it. For most of the year, living in Port Kydd was about just surviving. In the summers, the wet heat grew roaches the size of boxing mitts. On top of that there was always a sickness abound, something doctors called the Bonny Fever, and it came from old oyster shells and the constant wet of the soil and four hundred years of above-ground burials, and the further you went into summer, the hotter it got, so that the discomfort reached a point where you just couldn't take it anymore and had to throw a brick through a window. And winter was no better. Bone-breaking snows that flogged the city for weeks. Your toes never dried and it sent veterans—guys who'd wanted nothing more than dry socks—into fits of madness, recalling trenches along the Somme, leading some to loop a noose around a steam pipe. But in spring the city lied to you, told you tales. Elm blossoms and low necklines made you think you were living in a proper civilization. Everyone on the street—from your furnace workers to your mill girls—walked with a lightness. Even the guys who hadn't seen luck since the womb, the types falling out of the Catholic mission without a nickel to make a call, seemed to strut like men freshly fucked.

But that night, a low-simmering violence hung over the neighborhood. Joshua walked with his hat low and collar up and his gun ready to smile at the slightest noise. Two old men stepped out of the dark, each carrying something shiny and sharp. They gave Joshua a look over, and then let him pass. He cut south on Lancaster, with its five-story tenements, atop Irish taverns, Russian bathhouses, and Greek diners. He smelled the Bregenwurst from Fischer's biergarten and the remnants of coffee brewed in Ricci's café and the old urine and the spilled gin, all mixing into a miasma that made him feel at home. Immigration, shared poverty, governmental neglect, racism, anti-Papism, anti-Semitism, nativism, paranoia, and zoning laws were to blame for this Babel, one where a dozen languages mixed into a stew of noise so that you sometimes felt like all of your ancestors were arguing inside your damned head. The only people missing were Black. They lived up in Herhalling and never came downtown for reasons Joshua would rather not think of.

He crossed into Chinatown, his eyes fixed on the spider veins of the sidewalk, his skin warmed by laundry steam and oil barrel fires. The men wore short-brimmed hats and the women seemed to hide behind shut doors. Joshua bought a pork bun. The meat burnt his tongue, the chili fired his throat. He enjoyed it on the corner across from a curio shop. Two boys threw dice against a turned-over horse cart. An old man with an eye patch carried a washtub full of tilefish on his back. When he stopped to lay down his goods, he saw Joshua and kept walking. Meanwhile, everyone else looked the other way, passing cigarettes and stage whispers, performing, he figured, for his benefit. He felt for them, knew his own lot wasn't nearly as pained. This part of town was built on a landfill, the soft crust of the Earth formed by gravel, dirt, and the fossils of the first Port Kyddians. A couple of years back, the sleeping sickness had swept through and you could still see the survivors sitting on milk crates, barely awake, watching the sky for their spirits to return. A trio of tough boys pushed past, their hats low, and Joshua reached for his wallet. When he palmed it, he felt shamed for making these poor folks nervous, so he kept walking.

The sky had a starless, tar look about it, more than usual. The air smelled like burning kerosene. He passed the Smythe Waterworks, with its enormous Greek columns and wide pipes siphoning the river, and then cut through the edge of Cooke Village and her Bohemian cafes and three-story clapboard townhomes. Outside the Bassett Hotel, a man in a beret held a peacock by a leash, comforting the bird, because soon its neck would meet an axe, the rainbowed feathers plucked and sold to a haberdashery, while the meat made its way onto a porcelain plate. Soon he found himself in Tri-Town with her garment factories that only closed on Christmas, full of poor Polish girls bleeding their thumbs for a quarter an hour in the dark. There were no trees here, the elms, maples, and pines either chopped for cooking fires or dead from factory fumes. You'd find some turkey buzzards cutting a wide, majestic orbit overhead, waiting, Joshua thought, to feed upon some poor sucker.

He picked up his pace, all the while thinking about his sister. She'd only wanted to see if he was looking for work and made it seem like she was doing some kind of favor. And maybe that was all there was to the story. But, knowing Olive, there was usually a second or third angle that he had to worry over.

He considered this as he ended up in the Jewish Quarter, where the signs were all scribbled in Yiddish. He turned into an alley and stopped at a peeling green door. Down a ways, a little towheaded girl slept atop an empty potato sack. She wasn't more than ten, he thought, but you couldn't just eyeball kids for an age, not in this part of the city. There were a lot of stories for how she ended up in this alley and Joshua had heard them all—children dumped at the brothel, at the sweatshop, at the sea captain's feet. He didn't need to know her particular misery, so he peeked in his wallet, saw five bucks, and tried not to think of his own coming daughter. He glanced at the girl one more time before knocking on the door. The giant who opened up looked Joshua over and then glanced down the alley before letting him through.

The bar didn't have a name but you could tell that it used to be someone's home, from the mold-rotted mantle above the fireplace to the doorway where pencil marks denoted height and the words 'Stefan fünf.' Over in the kitchen they'd turned the counter into a bar and there was a man playing a guitar where the dining table should have stood. A peroxide blonde on the wrong side of pretty ran her hand down Joshua's lapel and when he shook his head 'no,' she told him to go jerk himself. Joshua got a glass of weak gin and then pushed through a sad, loaded crowd to get to a bedroom where five guys with prison postures sat at a card table. The pot was nickel and dime stakes so when he dropped a five they looked at him like Christmas come. He held his own for a little while, but by the tenth hand, when he'd gone all in on a flush, he got beat by a full house that hadn't come honest.

When he returned to the alley, the little girl had been replaced by a man in a navy suit, bent into a ball. Joshua looked around but there was no one coming or going, so when he went up to the man and asked if he needed anything, Joshua was hoping he didn't. He crouched and poked the man's chest. Still breathing. There were a few cars shooting down 14th and some people heading home from the taverns by foot, but everyone was looking straight ahead, minding their lane. He reached into the man's coat and found a wallet with fifteen bucks inside. He checked the man's hand. There were a couple of rings that slipped off quick, along with a watch that had the right time. The man's wingtips hadn't a scuff and his hat came from a nice shop up on Monroe Street. As he checked the label, the man's toupee slid off. On the top of his head, you could see a growth that looked like it could talk. A year or two left, maybe. Joshua straightened the toupee and then walked to a pawnshop. He figured he'd get ten dollars for the haul.

He got twenty-five.

CHAPTER TWO

Joshua awoke to a firm swat to the back of his skull. He raised his head from the piano, sheet music pasted to his cheek, a moldy taste in his mouth. Lily wore a silver nightgown and held the rolled-up newspaper like a blackjack. Her hair was short and bobbed, as black as the Crabbe Sound in winter, but not near as dark as the look she handed him.

"Good morning," she lied.

"You're lovely."

"Make me breakfast and I'll forgive you."

It was ten by the clock, but bar time ran fifteen minutes fast. He boiled water for coffee, and then scraped the griddle and cracked the eggs. He smelled the bologna, before laying it out to brown. She sat on the stool next to the potbelly, her eyes studying the food.

"We trapped in here all day?" he asked, while cutting mold off the cheese.

"Nah, the ice melted during your drunk."

It wasn't the first time she'd woken him with a smack. They'd been married two years and it was enough time for her to settle into their life, to see the good along with the bad, to get a sense

24

of what her next fifty years might look like. She was ambiva-
lent, he felt. After all, little girls didn't daydream about marry-
ing a barman who could throw pints back with the best Irish-
man, let alone men who had caused hurt and didn't own a bank
book. Yet she loved him, she professed over and over again, as if
she too could tell that he was skeptical of her feelings. But love
didn't fill the icebox, so he felt himself trying always to impress
her, because he always worried—despite her reassurances—that
she'd wake up wanting another life.

"How'd you sleep?" he asked.

"Orla kept me warm." Lily bit a piece of cheese and then
said, "I think she has fleas."

"Probably some worms too. Toughens her up."

"You're going to make a hell of a father."

It was this sort of banter that brought them together, the
constant tit-for-tat that made them look right, because from
the outside, you could have hardly picked a more asymmetrical
couple. While he was ginger and lumbering, she was all flapper
flash with a model's posture. She stood short in three-inch boots
and had a delicate figure that looked like it had never done a
hard day's work. And her clothes—even on their secondhand
budget—made trust funders stop for a second look. Spanish
heels and fringe dress that accentuated her sharp collar bones
and thin shoulders. Folks even sometimes asked if she was related to Louise Brooks. No one would guess she was a barman's
wife, and in many ways, she wasn't anyone's anything. She had
her own life. She worked part-time as a news photographer,
picking up stringer gigs from wire agencies and occasionally
snapping photos of debutante balls for the town's society pages.
It was that extra money that kept the Swill's lights on.

"I was kidding, Rivers," she said. "You're going to be great."

"Sorry, my mind…I was thinking…I'm just tired."

"Lay off the hard stuff for a few days, maybe?"

Chapter Two

"Yeah, you're right."

When she went up to the bathroom, he set the long table, putting out napkins and forks, and then plated the food. The kettle whistled and he poured it over the grounds, cowboy-style, and then snuck in a splash of whiskey. Upstairs, Lily picked up the ringing phone. He had a minute, so he took his coffee up to the street to find that spring had arrived. Under a warm sun, a streetcar rattled east, bound for the docks. Melting ice pooled in the cobblestone, and except for a few fallen elm branches, there was no sense anything at all had happened last night. Across the road, Styer's Bakery was humming, selling pumpernickel and rye to women pushing strollers. Down the way, Hiram's kosher butchery had opened its doors and Jessup's millinery already had a rack of red hats on the sidewalk. It was the sort of morning that made you forget the neighborhood was awash in bootleg, turning peaceful evenings into sloppy brawls. There were a couple of other speakeasies, places, like the Swill, with a green door to let everyone know their business. Most of these dives catered to a rougher crowd, guys just off ships, or other bruised-fist types looking for off-the-rack female company. The cops didn't care, not as long as you paid on time. Prohibition was something country preachers cared about. In Port Kydd, it was a just another excuse for the cops to extort you.

He stepped onto the sidewalk and turned to check his home for damage but saw nothing had changed. Like the rest of the Bonny, the Swill was three stories of faded brick, with three bays across, white window trims, and a low-hipped roof. It had been built on top of the remains of the old tavern, the first Swill, which legend said was destroyed during the riot of 1817. On the ground floor—above the bar—there was a bathroom and a dining room they never used. The second and third floors were made up of bedrooms, four in all. Back when his grandmother ran the bar, they used to keep boarders—salesmen passing through town, drifters who'd come to a standstill—but Joshua didn't like the idea of a stranger sleeping near his wife, even if it would have brought in a little extra money.

He took a drink of his coffee, tasted the bitter Irishness of it, and then saw Simon Green, the iceman, making his way from the docks. He was driving a pair of old nags who pulled the ice truck like it was still 1900. Fords and motorbuses honked as they passed, their drivers cursing, but Simon kept his eyes on the road while cropping his team, Hercules and Ethel. Joshua ducked back into the Swill and locked the door. He owed the iceman seven dollars.

Downstairs, Lily hunched over her plate, shoveling food. He sat beside her, took a small bite, felt sick, and then passed the rest to her.

"Thank you," she said, starting in on his plate. "Might be home late tonight."

"New boyfriend?"

"I can't help it. Morning sickness just tells the boys that a girl is easy."

"We're savages," he said. "Where are you really going?"

"Seeing O'Neil's new play with Rose." Rose was her sister. She didn't like Joshua. "Don't worry about the money. She paid. It's five hours long."

"Five hours?" he said. "What the hell's it about?"

"The War and insanity."

"Lovely. Who called?"

"Oh, right, Rafael wants you to drop by."

Joshua lit a cigarette.

"What aren't you telling me?" Lily asked.

He took another drag, thought for a moment, but there wasn't a good lie to tell.

"Olive dropped in last night. Just for a minute," he said. "Heard you were pregnant."

She took a drink of coffee, and then mumbled, "How much did you give her?"

He got up and went back to the kitchen for more coffee.

"Don't get mad," she said. "You're the one keeping things from me."

"She didn't ask and I don't have a spare dollar even if she did." When he came back from the kitchen, she reached for his hand.

"We'll be fine," she said. "Things will pick up."

He didn't think so. By his count, they had forty dollars in a shoebox upstairs, fifteen in the till, and the forty he'd made last night. He owed at least a hundred dollars to various people in the neighborhood and the cops expected twenty-five bucks at the end of the month. He'd have to pawn something to make it to April.

"What did she really want?" Lily said.

"Just to say hello," Joshua said.

"Save the fairy tales for Sunday." Lily looked down at their medium-rare child. "Someday you're going to have to visit your Aunt Olive in the pokey. We'll bring fruitcake with a nail-file baked into it."

CHAPTER THREE

Rafael Castillo sat on his stoop holding a tea mug and a book. He wore old time leather suspenders, a crisp white shirt, blue trousers, and black boots, polished clean. His skin was a shade lighter than brown, his posture straight, and his hair only just turning to ash in this, his 81st year. He was handsome for an old man. Not the beauty of his youth but a man you'd call distinguished. In a way, it was a natural disguise. No one would look at him and guess that he was about as tough a man as had ever stepped foot on the Island. Years ago, alongside his wife Lucy, Rafael had worked as a smuggler, taking his boat out beyond the Sound to meet steamers approaching from Europe, ships full of foreign goods and owners who didn't want to pay the customs tax or get busted by the Comstock men. You name it, Rafael and Lucy had smuggled it: bridal gowns, condoms, hats, cigars, watches, sugar, bay oil, pearls, silkworms, silverware, diamonds, stockings, guns, booze, and diaphragms. On flush days, he was the most popular man in the Bonny but there was always someone trying to chisel into his trade and those men lived, or didn't live, to regret it. But that was all over with now. When Lucy died ten years earlier, Rafael had scuttled their boat and taken up the writing of his memoirs. Still, even in retirement, when he told someone to drop by, they always did.

Rafael shut his book to look Joshua over.

"My friend, you look old today."

"Yep," Joshua said. "And it isn't getting any better. What are you reading?"

"You do not care."

"I don't. Looks thick though."

"Some men have much to say."

He followed Rafael into his townhome. It had been a brothel after the Civil War and you could tell from the plush red carpeting and knockers on the bedroom doors. Rafael said he won the house in a card game, but Joshua knew he'd inherited it from the old madam who'd had a soft spot for him. When Joshua stepped into the entranceway, he was greeted by a suit of armor standing before a map of Mexican California, circa 1840. A very old, very sharp Italian saber hung beside it. Rafael had named it *Collette*. In the parlor, tapestries of Spanish royalty hung along the wood paneled walls, while over by the bookshelves, Rafael kept a rack of fine Spanish wines. While Rafael headed to the kitchen, Joshua went to the window and pulled back the curtain. A pair of street urchins chased a mutt down the street. When the dog stopped on top of an old coat, the girl shooed it away, while the boy searched the coat, finding a couple of coins and a bag of tobacco.

When Rafael returned with the coffee, he said, "There is a rumor that Roche is passing into town."

Joshua nodded.

"You understand, of course, that even the lowest rat looks upon Roche with disgust?"

"If you don't deal with those types, you aren't dealing," Joshua said.

Chapter Three

Rafael sat on a brass-gilded chair, like something out of Versailles, and then let his cup rest on his lap. He didn't move like most old men, wasn't clumsy or groaning but at peace with his body. He was slower, for sure, but you always got the feeling he could still drop you with a right cross. Rafael claimed that a lifetime of fine food and wine kept up his vigor.

"What's the matter?" Joshua asked. "Why didn't you just come by?"

"Your wife does not see your sister in—how do you say it—in a favorable light. And I have not lived this long by making enemies of men's wives."

Joshua had hoped Olive really had just stopped by for a visit but he wasn't surprised there was more to it.

"Yesterday, I had the unfortunate fortune of finding myself in conversation with that vile pagan Joel Vanderhock," Rafael said. "He asked after your sister. I did not like the way he phrased the question so I broke his thumb. There were many tears that followed. Do you know why he would wish to speak to her?"

"I don't know." Vanderhock was a local preacher who dabbled in extortion and bootlegging. Maybe Olive had stolen from him. If that was the case, she was in trouble. Vanderhock wasn't someone you could push around and not expect consequences. He was a blowhard, for sure, but also a scary man.

"She came by last night," Joshua said. He described Olive's visit and her offer of a job. Unlike with Lily, he didn't leave anything out.

Rafael went over to the corner by an old globe, one from 1800, and spun it. "I cannot believe she wishes your assistance in the commandeering of a Wells Fargo wagon."

"Didn't say but she was talking about paintings."

"Ah, yes. The arts are always there to cause one trouble. I told your grandmother as much." Rafael went to the kitchen and returned with a bowl of pistachios. "Are you considering her offer?"

Joshua broke open a nut, the pink of the shell staining his fingers, and admitted that he'd been running short lately, that he was thinking of heading out on the road, maybe finding some work in California.

"There's this town called Ventura, just outside of Los Angeles," Joshua said. "It's a quiet place, peaceful. Was there moving some bootleg around '22, '23. There are these islands out there. No one lives on them. You can stand on the cliffs and see whales swimming and dolphins jumping. A man could get a boat, ferry sightseers, make a quiet living."

"Ah, California, the most beautiful land in the world before the infernal *yanquis* invaded." Rafael's gaze drifted toward the globe. He'd been born outside San Francisco before it was called San Francisco but hadn't returned to the state for over sixty years. "The City of San Buenaventura it was once called. I can imagine it a lovely home for a bachelor."

Joshua didn't know what he meant. Lily was adventurous, a girl who pushed back against her parents when they didn't want her to marry him. California might be what she needed.

"Your mother did not raise a fool," Rafael said. "If Lily were to abandon the Island, she should wither and die like a fruit devoid of water."

Maybe, Joshua thought. But what choices did they have left? "She hasn't tried it yet."

"I do not know of your island of whales of which you romanticize, but if she were to go, they shall check her for horns and argue that she crucified the baby Jesus."

"The Bonny is no place to raise a kid."

"It never was." Rafael lowered his gaze, head shaking, as if he were trying to resurrect a memory. "It is a filthy land devoid of culture and honor, but your family has done well by that tavern and it would be a shame to see it dissolve like every other fine establishment worth a two-dollar whore in this city."

"Some things get old and die."

"Only if you allow it."

When they returned to the street, they found a band of cops loading a Slav woman into a Paddy wagon. Her broken nose dripped blood onto her sarafan. Nearby a few old timers passed a bottle just outside of John Shepard's tavern, the sort of place that opened at 6am for the morning drinking rush. And this is where he was going to raise his daughter? He loved the bar and he loved parts of the Bonny, but you could only keep your head in the ground for so long before the ground bit back.

Rafael sighed. "Joshua, you know I love your sister, correct? I was present on the day of her birth. And I understand that she is the only blood you have that remains, but she never met a truth she couldn't spin into fiction. Remember, you have more significant problems—so be wary. Sometimes even the people we love must go down."

CHAPTER FOUR

When he got back to the Swill it was nearly noon and Lily had gone ahead and set up the bar—putting down the chairs and scattering sawdust, while also keeping an eye on the potato soup. He kissed her cheek, while she sang to herself, shimmying to a jangly tune he didn't know.

"You seem happy."

"Look at these," she said, pulling out a sheaf of photographs. "Tell me what you think."

He tried to smile in a way that looked sincere but knew came off as phony. When she showed him her pictures, he had no idea how to respond except through general praise. That one's good. This one is good. This last one might be better. It was all he could say. While she made most of her money working for the women's pages, she also liked to wander the streets, snapping pictures of people in the Marble Graveyard, or down by the docks, or in front of one of Port Kydd's antebellum buildings, contrasting the modernity of her subjects with the decaying infrastructure. She'd sold a few to some artier publications, but Joshua couldn't imagine paying more than a nickel for any of them.

Chapter Four

Along the bar, she arranged a dozen photographs. The arches and stonework put it at the Port Kydd Veteran's Lodge. He'd passed by it a hundred times without ever stepping inside. The first pictures showed a trio of old men, Civil War vets, dressed in frayed blue overcoats, each haggard in the eyes and tubercular around the mouth, ninety years old at the youngest, the last witnesses to that conflict now reduced to waiting for that first morning drink. Remarkable, Joshua thought, that they could stand living that long. One wore a medal in the shape of a star and Joshua remembered similar ones on Decoration Day, when the Port Kydd 29th marched down Bonny Lane, a wave of limping blue bracketed by cheering crowds. They'd stopped the parade after the last war.

You could see why with the next pictures. In a wide room, eagles carved into the stonework and the flag hanging above the bar, there was a pair of men about Joshua's age stroking their pints, eyes as far from her camera as the room allowed.

"I tried flirting and even told a dirty joke, you know the one about the blonde and the magic goat, but they just told me to shove off," she said. "Actually, they called me a name that rhymes with clucking witch."

Neither of the soldiers had all the limbs their mothers had made for them, one missing his left arm below the elbow, the second, a foot. After a while he couldn't look anymore so he focused on the bar itself and thought about nothing.

"Seriously, Rivers, what do you think? There's something heartbreaking about them, right?"

He went to the kitchen, tasted the soup, put a little salt in it, lowered the flame, and then returned to the bar, where he reached, right above the rail whiskey, for his army revolver.

"Is that really necessary?" Lily said.

"You never know until you do."

Chapter Four

She followed him into the kitchen, past the pantry, before stopping beside the icebox. Next to it was a door that looked like a utility closet. He pulled it open and stepped into the darkness. Lily handed him the flashlight.

"You didn't say if you liked the pictures," she said.

He stopped at a stone staircase that fell down into the dark. He smelled the sea, heard the water lapping below. Even with the light, it was difficult to balance, so he ran his hands along the mossy bedrock.

"Maybe you should stay upstairs," he said.

"I'm fine. Used to be a ballerina."

"I'll try to imagine that later."

"I was seven."

"Now you've gone and ruined it."

With the first step, he felt the slickness of the stone.

"We should wire this for light someday," Lily said.

"Nah. Don't want some electric company stooge following a red wire down here."

"What did you think of the pictures, really?"

"They're good."

"Liar."

On the landing, the flashlight made clear the enormity of the cavern, which stretched two stories up and thirty yards across, enough to get a few skiffs through side by side. The dark water was empty except for a tire floating past.

"I love it down here," Lily said. "You know almost no one in the city knows about these tunnels. I didn't until I met you."

It was an underground river system, formed with creation, a refuge for smugglers and the down and out. The caverns crisscrossed beneath the east side of town, twisting north from Chinatown all the way up to Lancaster Park. Sometimes one caved in and a street would fall into the water and a few people followed into the abyss but no one thought twice about it, no one wondered about the world under their feet.

"Do you think Roche's bringing another girlfriend with him?" Lily said. "They're always so pretty."

"Is it a girlfriend if you pay her?"

Lily pointed down the channel. "I see a light."

Roche rowed down the waterway like a gondolier, using a long staff to push his cigarette boat, while keeping his outboard idled, better to not stir up the water and what may lie beneath. A woman at the bow held a lantern and was dressed, as Joshua figured, like a tart, her pink garter showing beneath her white skirt and a tattoo of a shamrock on her left breast. But Lily was right. The girl was pretty. Roche, on the other hand, was a squirmy little shit, with his greasy mustache, sandalwood cologne, and too-tight turtleneck that showed off his rubbery midriff whenever he lifted the staff.

"Monsieur Rivers," Roche said. He tossed Joshua a line to tie off. "And Mademoiselle."

Roche hopped onto the dock and helped his friend off the skiff. The girl teetered in her heels and then shook away Roche's hand.

"May I introduce the beautiful Thelma. Thelma, this is the family Rivers of the Bonnyville."

Thelma spit snuff into the channel. Charm school, Joshua thought.

"You make us sound like royalty, Roche," Lily said.

"You are a Cleopatra amongst the mob of serfs. I would be your Mark Antony if not for my loyalty to Monsieur Rivers."

Joshua grunted. Guys like Roche gave him lockjaw. They talked until their faces turned red, flirting with your wife in fancy words while also professing friendship.

Joshua leaned over the side to get a look at the goods. There was a crate marked "Whooping Cough Syrup," which was

Joshua's usual order of cheap gin and bourbon. But alongside sat another crate marked "Canadian Club." If Roche hadn't bothered with a fake name, it meant this was the good stuff, straight from Windsor.

"How much for the good whiskey?" Joshua asked.

"Oh, I'm so sorry Monsieur Rivers, but that has been promised to the Ark Royal Club. If I had known you were in the market for the finest of my goods, it would be of course yours for the taking, but I have seen the Swill's clientele and thought otherwise."

The Ark Royal Club was a posh joint with a coat and tie policy, a chandelier that got dusted every day, and a big brass band full of Black musicians who weren't allowed at the bar.

"But do not distress," Roche said. "Roche has not forgotten his old friends. Never shall he forget his old friends. Loyalty. That is the essence of my very soul, the code by . . . by which I live by. Without loyalty we are no better than beasts of prey. Savages. It is what separates us from the lowest mongrel. Honor and loyalty, yes. Friendship. You can count on Roche for that."

Roche had burned a dozen customers over the years with the cops or a local mob. The Swill, Joshua figured, wasn't worth his time yet.

"I'll want the Canadian Club," Joshua said. "How much is the Ark Royal paying?"

"Joshua, we can't," Lily said.

"Don't worry. We did well last night."

"I don't know," Lily said.

Meanwhile, Roche said nothing. He was figuring out how much money he could screw out of his "old friend."

"Thirty," Roche said. "But the Ark Royal will be very upset with me."

"They'll manage," Joshua said.

CHAPTER FIVE

The radio came in clipped, static ridden. White noise with a beat. Every third word cut. So you had to piece it together, pay attention. It was the curse of the basement bar in the early 20th century. Joshua twisted the dial to the news.

The grand jury was still out on Al Capone.

Mussolini's party won re-election with 98% of the vote.

And 100,000 Parisians lined up to pay respects to General Ferdinand Foch who lay in waiting under the Arc de Triomphe. Joshua remembered catching a glimpse of the Gènèralissime in the days following the Second Battle of Saint-Mihiel. The old man's uniform had been clean, his hair washed, free of lice. He was the "hero" of the War, the radio kept saying.

It was just past ten and Lily was still at the five-hour play, so Joshua poured another drink and looked over the front of the house. At the long table there was an old poet named Jacobs, who kept trim muttonchops and wrote epic verses about Sir Walter Raleigh. He played poker with Jack Healey, who made a living killing rats, and Miguel Santos, a Mexican tailor who'd come north to escape the Revolution. Over by the piano Shauna Kelly, an out-of-work burlesque dancer, listened to Marjorie O'Neil reminisce about her dead boy.

"I was proud, my boy was a soldier," Marjorie said. "A real man."

Joshua thought about the possibility of a son and decided he'd cut off one of the boy's toes before letting him carry a gun for the government.

"All the real men are dead," Shauna said. "Or married."

And, finally, there was the Stranger at the end of the bar, reading a book. He was an older man with blonde curly hair and a western feel about him from his calfskin coat down to his cowboy boots. He'd come in an hour earlier, asked for whiskey, and had hardly looked at it until Joshua came over to ask after him.

"Only Canadians could come up with a drink so boring," the Stranger said, raising his glass. "It's a sad state of man when you find yourself relieved to be drinking swill like this, pun intended, of course."

"Haven't heard it a million times."

The Stranger took a long drink, before turning to the barroom. "Feel as though I should toast this place. You see she's one of my five favorite drinking holes on this Earth, and, son, I've been inside every last one of them, from here to Budapest and back to Bangkok. This was long before you found your way behind the bar."

"I was born upstairs."

"Long before then as well. Came through town near fifty years ago along with my girl, looking for work. The kind you'd expect from a young man with no compunction about church morality."

Thug? Thief? Killer? It was hard to tell with old men, especially when their eyes were wrung red and hard. Yet Joshua didn't feel threatened. He'd known men like this all of his life, old timers who pained to stand up straight and once in a while stopped short to shake from their heads a memory of hurt caused or endured.

Chapter Five

Joshua was thinking on this when the front door opened and down the steps came two young men, no more than sixteen a piece, each wearing black church clothes. The second boy was of no consequence, a cousin to the first, but that first was trouble. His name was Willie Vanderhock, and, along with his black suit, he wore a minister's collar two sizes too large, so that it dangled from his neck like a manacle. He was an odd one—pimpled and without humor, the sort of grave little shit his family bred in trios. His sole ambition, as far as Joshua could tell, was to one day take his father's place as a preacher to Little Holland. He and his cousin stopped at the other end of the bar and folded their hands, as if afraid to touch anything lest they be struck down by lightening.

"Hey Willie," Joshua said. "Want a drink?"

"Ale is the devil's brew."

Joshua lit a cigarette and blew it in the boy's direction. "Got a girlfriend yet?"

Willie unfolded his hands and held his palms up like he was waiting for stigmata.

"The Reverend Joel Vanderhock requests your presence at his church, tomorrow."

"How is your dad?"

"Tomorrow."

"Not when I have a free moment? It's a busy day Willie. I've got some stock deals in the works and then a gala in the evening. Got to get the tux pressed."

Down the bar, the Stranger laughed. He raised his glass to Willie before taking down the last of it.

"You're a low sort, Mr. Rivers," Willie said.

"Don't you people pray for my type?" Joshua said.

"Only for those worthy of forgiveness."

Joshua excused himself and went to the kitchen and glanced at the warm, empty icebox. He knew someday the Vanderhocks would come calling, asking for an "offering" in order to keep the Swill from burning down. That was the reverend's game. Over the last decade, Vanderhock had pushed out the mobs and brought a level of peace to the Bonny, but it all came with a price for protection. You didn't pay on time, then someone in their church clothes would throw a torch through your window.

When Joshua returned to the barroom, he was intent on talking about all of his troubles, about how broke he was, about the baby, about the admiration he had for the Reverend Vanderhock's good works, but stopped when he found Willie faced away, as still as a daguerreotype.

"Cheer up," Joshua said. "The end times probably aren't starting before midnight."

But Willie wasn't paying him any mind. Shauna had lifted her leg onto the long table, dress hiked to her hips, pointing to Miguel where her stocking was fraying. It was a very nice leg.

"These garments are very difficult to repair," Miguel said. "Very delicate. Best buy a new one."

"Oh, honey, if I had that kind of money, I wouldn't be drinking here."

This was exactly the sort of debauchery Willie's congregation condemned. He put his hands together to pray yet couldn't bring himself to look elsewhere. Shauna felt the boy's stare.

"How you doing kid?" Shauna said. "Got something in your eye?"

"No, it's not—" Willie said and then turned to Joshua and sneered. "Before sundown if possible, and if not, make it possible."

He ran up the stairs like Joshua had pulled a gun, slamming the door hard enough to get Orla growling.

"Guessing by your face," the Stranger said, "his arrival portends difficult times ahead."

Joshua nodded. "The Church of the Holy Bagman."

"Ah, yes. Difficult times," the Stranger said. "Meant to ask earlier. There used to be a pretty lady with a little girl running this place."

"Fifty years ago, you say? My grandmother and mother then."

"Your ma still around?"

"She passed in '05."

The Stranger nodded but not too long. Dead mothers were an old story. The Stranger reached up to the rafters, extending his fingers, rubbing the beams back and forth. "Old wood," he said. "Her mother alive to see that?"

"Yeah."

"A shame to outlive your children. Been fortunate thus far. Both my kids are still breathing, though I've got a boy whose head's full of stupid at times. Children?"

"In the fall."

The Stranger raised his glass. "Cheers."

When they clinked glasses, Joshua peeked at the Stranger's book: *Red Harvest* by Dashiell Hammett. He'd never heard of it. Before he could ask after it, Shauna called him over for another round. He returned to find the Stranger petting Orla.

"Same dog? Must be losing the last of my goddamn mind."

"No. But they all look the same," Joshua said. "So what brings you back here?"

"My girl and I are passing through and she went out to see some terribly long play, so I thought I'd stop in for a little drink and a little memory in the meantime."

"Same girl?"

"Remarkably, yes."

Joshua raised his glass. "Cheers."

The Stranger went to the end of the bar and ran his hands along the wood. "Let me see, let me see, oh, yes."

He pointed at a long scratch that stretched the width of the wood, a scar that had been there for as long as Joshua could remember.

"Was here when this happened."

"Were you now?" Joshua took the rest of his drink and then reached for the bottle.

"You see a man, an old man with white hair came into the bar. He went up to this other fellow, a Spaniard with a sword. You know of him?"

"I do."

"Now I imagine you get all kinds in here, but the Spaniard was like no one I had ever seen. Beautiful, in a way strange for a man. Well, the long and short of it is that words were exchanged over a mutual acquaintance, the old man's son, I believe. He said something cruel to the Spaniard."

"What was it?"

"'You killed my boy.' Well, the Spaniard took out his sword, but rather than gutting the white-haired man, he instead cut deep into this bar. Upset your grandmother fiercely. She passed some impolite words. And that's how you got this scratch in the bar."

Joshua would ask Rafael about it the next time he saw the old man.

"Good story."

"Not quite done yet," the Stranger said, holding up his hand. "Here's the odd part. There was an old woman in the back. Couldn't quite tell where her people come from. Well, she just materializes like she'd stepped into a man's dream, and comes up to the white-haired man, lays her hand upon his face, and says he must apologize. Well, I was expecting the white-haired man to scoff, but instead he did something quite remarkable. He knelt and asked for said forgiveness. About the most mystical moment of my whole damn life."

Joshua took another look at the scratch, running his finger along the ridge, before shutting his eyes and seeing the faces he could only imagine because it was a time that occurred fifteen years before his birth, and fifteen years in the Bonny aged a man in dog years. His mother before she was sick. His grandmother before she was bitter. Rafael before...well, Rafael was probably the same, just a bit quicker back then. He'd worried the Stranger's story would resurrect a melancholy from recalling the dead and the nearly dead but it had made him grateful.

"Thank you."

The Stranger nodded just as the door opened and down the stairs came two women. The first was Lily wearing a feathery hat and a queasy expression. Her morning sickness generally arrived around midnight, which old ladies said foretold a hell-bent child, the kind in need of a long nap in a jail cell out on Flywell Island. The second woman was in her 60s with long dark hair and what looked like an old scar down the side of her face. She went to the Stranger and kissed him.

"Why are you still down here, you sentimental old coot?"

"You went and answered your own question," the Stranger said.

Joshua went to Lily, but she turned, her eyes faint, and he reached to steady her.

"You got any soup and crackers?" she said.

"Get it right up. How was the play?"

"Long and sad." She leaned against him and groaned. "How was your night?"

"It's strange, I just heard the oddest story." He turned, but the Stranger and his girl had disappeared, leaving behind a ten-dollar bill.

"What was it?" Lily said. "What's the story?"

"Just," he said. "Just about my grandmother and Rafael."

"Your grandmother? What about her?"

"Oh, you know—"

"I don't," Lily said. "You never talk about her."

CHAPTER SIX

In Port Kydd, the ladybugs swarm like cicadas. They rise out of the soil every seven years to mate in elms and ivy, but, in a city of concrete, they've evolved to invade homes, living in harmony with the cockroaches, each taking up tenancy inside of ovens and bureaus, sleeves and hair. Mystics called them harbingers of death, a bearer of sickness, a forecast of bloodshed. Joshua didn't believe any of it. To him, there was no such thing as prophecy or fate. Bad things just happened, usually from stupidity. And the ladybugs were no more than an annoyance. He'd woken early to sweep the dead off the barroom floor. The ladybugs in spring, his grandmother used to say, meant passenger pigeons in winter. But, of course, those birds were all dead now.

That morning didn't feel right to Joshua. When Lily came down as he prepped the kitchen—slicing just enough bread and pickles, liverwurst, and cheese, to feed twenty—his hands felt like paws. He dropped the knife twice, knocked over a ramekin of mustard, and felt the onion juice burning in the cracks of his hands. Lily turned on the radio, hoping to jazz the place up a bit, but somehow the music just made it feel even more glum. At noon a pair of old men wearing matching bowlers stopped in to sit quiet over mugs of stout. A trio of coeds followed, stinking of old Collier Park money. In their smart sweaters and ten-cent words, they came across like anthropologists scouting the natives of the Amazon. They turned down the lunch plate, only to accept a gin fizz.

"Don't drink too many," Lily said. "Otherwise you'll awake with an Irish baby in your belly. It's why I work here now."

By one, the bar was empty. Lily blamed the ladybugs. "If I didn't live above a bar, I'd drink at home."

In the kitchen, Joshua wiped down the griddle and the pans and the cutting board. He daydreamed about getting a piano player to come in twice a week, maybe someone who'd work for tips, perhaps someone who played a bit upbeat, who could sing. Perhaps a girl with nice legs. He kept thinking this way—how to drum up business—when he heard a voice from the front of the house.

He stopped beside Lily, before dropping his rag at the sight of a man leaning at the end of the bar, elbow near the taps, a bulge in his navy coat. Joshua had seen this man a thousand times, always in uniform, a rifle in hand. This one was in his late thirties, clean-shaven, with blonde hair, and shoulders back like a soldier's. The big blue eyes gave him a sort of Buster Keaton look if Buster Keaton was a hired gun.

"I am Mister Hess." He paused to swat a ladybug off his coat. "And you are Mister Joshua Rivers of 214 East Smythe Street, yes?"

He spoke English like he'd learned it in Ohio, quite recently.

"Yes, correct?" Hess asked.

Up on the street, two men yelled in Italian, their voices gradually pitching higher until they sounded like cats mating. Joshua felt a breeze coming through the door, heard air popping in the steam pipes.

"It is a comely day," Hess went on. "Much too comely to find oneself in a murky tavern such as this, don't you think?"

Chapter Six

"Not buying a mansion off today's take."

"No, no mansion for you. Or me. We are workingmen. Commoners. We work for gentry and gentry give us enough so we can feed our families but not so much that we can rise up and cut off their thumbs. You know this is correct, yes?"

"Own this place free and clear. Don't work for anyone."

"That is true only in literal sense," Hess said, turning, smiling at Lily, who flicked her eyes toward Joshua. She was scared.

"You have offered me no drink. Rude is the word."

"We're closed," Joshua said.

"It is no matter. Myself, I do not indulge in drink. I prefer walk in the woods, swim in cold of the lake. Austrian men are a men who drink too much lager. They turn fat, lazy. It is why we are no longer empire. It is good in this country that you have this prohibition. Now you do not offer drink or introduce me to your wife Missus Lily Rivers and that is rude."

Before Joshua could answer, Hess flipped open a notebook, and then read, "Formerly Lillian Rebekah Stern, age 28, born in Jewish Quarter neighborhood...hmm...graduate Port Kydd Women's College, newspaper photographer, arrested June 22nd, 1925 for disorderly conduct, charges dropped, arrested September 30, 1926, simple assault, charges dropped, married July 1st, 1927. Odd. Anniversary of Somme Battle, a very bad day for English side. I have a very good day that day and become hero."

Hess shut his notebook and then said, "And you Mister Rivers, Joshua Rivers, you are a very tough man. I know of your travels throughout this very large country, many faces you have taken on, and I know, of course, of your record during war. I do believe you have shoebox full of your medals. Perhaps bag of German ears."

"Lily can you go check on the soup for me?"

"I think it better if she stays."

She folded her hands across her stomach.

"Now I am not here to frighten," Hess said. "That is not my intent, to escalate. I am here for your sister, Olive, a ridiculous name, a fruit to make oil."

"Fucking hell," Lily said.

Hess smiled. "In Austria wives are be beaten for foul words."

"She isn't here."

"I very much need to speak to her, for my employer. You see I work for rich man directly, unlike you, who does it through osmosis."

"That's a pretty big word, osmosis."

"It is amazing what one will pick up when they listen. American people talk too much. Fear silence. Now, your sister, where may I find her?"

"Sorry, pal. Haven't seen Olive in over a year."

"Joshua," Lily said.

He shot his eyes toward her.

"I think you see her more recent than that," Hess said.

"You might want to try your luck over in Pinebox Square," Joshua said.

Hess dropped his cigarette and mashed it out on the sawdust. "Those are places of degeneration, filth. The women—"

He lingered on Lily for a moment, before tipping his hat and taking his time up the stairs.

When Hess was gone, Joshua pointed down at a latch in the floorboards. If you pulled it, you lifted the door to a dugout, one that had been built with the bar. He used it to store milk when he couldn't pay for ice. But now he saw another reason for it.

"If you ever see that man again," Joshua said. "Hide."

Lily whacked him across the chest, hard enough to wake the dog.

"Your loony sister," she said.

"What do you want me to say?"

"That's not the goddamn point and you know it."

CHAPTER SEVEN

By mid-afternoon they'd settled into a sour silence, Joshua scraping mildew from the caulking around the bar sink, while Lily sat at the long table, looking over her photographs. This was how they fought, a big blow followed by a long, bitter quiet. He knew she wasn't entirely wrong. Olive brought trouble wherever she hung her hat. It was nothing to worry over, he thought, but then the door opened and he reached for his gun.

Lily smirked, like it somehow proved her point.

There was no need for firearms because it was just old Miss Amand. She stopped on the landing, adjusting her green hat, prim-like, and then went to her usual stool, right by the kitchen. Her hair was gray and her skin weathered and dark but not Black or Mexican or even Italian dark. It was something specific to her, a color that seemed to change in the light and shadows, from one season to the next, so that it was near impossible to pinpoint where her people came from. Rafael believed she was Moldavian. Lily thought Flemish. Others said Abyssinian or Phoenician or Sumerian. When you asked directly, Miss Amand smiled and somehow you forgot the question.

"What's the good news, Miss Amand?" he asked.

"We are still a fundamentally generous people," she said, taking off her riding gloves. "And I won a fifty-dollar trifecta."

"Glad to see the gods are favoring you."

"Gods, ha. The Gods do me no good, a throng of prima donnas. No, a friendly groom whispered that the jockey riding Queen's Consort was giving his steed a little pick-me-up. Seven to one in the ninth race. Best money I've ever spent."

As Joshua pulled the cask, Lily unpacked a sheaf of photographs, ones she hadn't bothered to show him. A couple of days earlier, she'd wandered down near the old stockyards, her camera eyeballing anything ramshackle. She leafed through the pictures of the Old Courthouse, the Wagon Wheel Tavern, and the Negro Cemetery before stopping at a photo taken outside of Washington's Fort, which, lately, some had been using as a dope palace.

"I'm especially fond of this one, dear," Miss Amand said.

In it, a tuxedoed drunk slept outside the fort's doors, two-hundred-year-old brick at his back, while his tasseled and short-skirted girlfriend laid prostrate across his legs.

"Used to be the citizens would punish such wanton idleness by stripping these dunderheads of every cent they had on them." Miss Amand raised the photograph to the light. "You should hang it up here."

Lily looked around at the portraits of long dead politicians and poets.

"No," Lily said. "Too contemporary."

"Ah, nonsense," Miss Amand said. "Back in the old days, Joshua's grandmother hung lovely paintings done by her own hand, harsh and beautiful art that reawakened the humors of this old tavern, balancing the choleric with the sanguine."

"What do you think?" Lily asked Joshua.

He didn't know. It had always been his grandmother's decision and, five years after her death, he still felt more like he hadn't the right.

"You do have the right," Miss Amand said, though he hadn't spoken. "It's your tavern, now."

It was half his, he wanted to correct her.

"Whatever you want," he said to Lily. "I like your pictures."

"You say you do," Lily said. "But I don't believe you."

He was about to say something resembling a lie when St. Nicholas' struck three bells and gave him an excuse to fetch his coat and hat.

"Don't be mad," Lily said. "I just think you humor me."

"It's not that. Should go see Vanderhock during the lull. Get this over with."

At the drop of the reverend's name, Miss Amand spit.

"Dogs, all of them," Miss Amand said. "Should have drowned that seed on the eighth day of creation."

She was right but he didn't like her scaring Lily.

"Are you sure you should go?" Lily asked.

He slipped his gun into his coat.

"I'll be careful."

CHAPTER EIGHT

Joel Vanderhock operated out of the Church for Messianic Return down in Little Holland, the old Dutch neighborhood, which had been reduced to a couple square blocks hawking wooden clogs and windmill kitsch. The buildings—mostly five story walkups—were built of gray brick with Juliet porches bearding the windows. A few still flew the Dutch tricolors as if the town hadn't cast aside the name New Rotterdam nearly three centuries earlier. Joel was the black heart of the neighborhood, leading a congregation of ex-hopheads, retread call girls, and broken prizefighters, each seeking salvation before the end of times. You'd find the congregation's stink all over town, picketing so-called dens of iniquity like speakeasies, brothels, and gambling halls. On Sundays, Joel gave fiery sermons about the Four Horsemen of the Apocalypse coming to cleanse this Sodom. Afterwards, he sold communion wine by the gallon. It all made him a very nice living.

Joshua stopped on the corner to look at the parish built of gray fieldstone with a steeple stained by coal smoke. If you weren't from here, you'd think it was a quaint little sanctuary for the good word, but Joshua knew it stunk of the sort of grift charlatans like Joel and his family had pushed on the neighborhood for centuries. There was a rectory out back where he kept his offices, and in every corner of the church you'd find a collection plate alongside some heel "asking" for donations. Any crook on the down and out could find work here as one of God's chosen tough guys.

The one waiting at the door was a serious young man dressed in a flashy blue suit, slick black hair, and tortoiseshell glasses. Beneath the lenses, the boy wore the eyes of a convert, unwilling to blink in case rapture came and went in that split second. Yet his manner—balled up fists and welterweight shoulders—was all hoodlum.

He shoved a flyer into Joshua's gut.

The End is Near: Repent and forego the luxuries of this world for the Lord's train has no baggage compartment.

"Nice suit," Joshua told him. "Your boss here?"

The boy cracked his knuckles to look Joshua over, saw nothing that scared him and then nodded toward the church.

"He's in the back," the boy said. "He's armed too."

"This isn't a stick-up," Joshua said. "We're old friends."

"He ain't got friends."

The church had simple hardwood pews, a plain unadorned altar, and an enormous cross that made Jesus appear like one of Barnum's giants. Candles burned in the corners and a few old ladies knelt beside them, praying—if Joshua had to guess—for their wayward children. He went behind the cross, through a back hall, where he could already hear the boil of Joel's percolating snake oil.

Joshua stopped in the doorway, while Joel chatted with a fat man in a double-breasted suit who wore a toothbrush mustache flecked gray. The man kept an old-fashioned derby on his lap and a gold pocket watch chain hung from his coat. He checked his watch and then gave a long, forced yawn.

Chapter Eight

"So we've come to an understanding," Joel said. "A détente."

"That's not the word you mean," the fat man said.

"Covenant, how's that smart guy?" Joel saw Joshua and pointed. "This is Rivers. He comes from a long line of thieves, spies, and scoundrels."

"Unlike Joel here," Joshua said, "whose family of nobles stretches back to the Island's Indian days."

"We do," Joel said. "We do at that."

The fat man stood without giving Joshua a first look.

"I am acquainted with your family's long history on Smythe Street."

Joshua had no idea who he was and no one was passing out introductions. The fat man looked back at Joel with a cool gaze, while Joel went red in the face. Despite the church, Joel never acquired the even-tempered demeanor that came with doing God's work. He was 50-ish, squishy, with a dry, flaking face. What you couldn't tell by looking at him was that Joel was fairly shrewd, the sort of guy who looked more checkers than chess but knew enough to define a gambit. Still, his left hand was in a cast, just as Rafael promised.

"The terms hold," Joel said.

"We're gentlemen. There's no need to spit on our palms like savages."

This guy must have had pull, Joshua thought, otherwise Joel would have had a couple of his boys take him down to the Sound for working his mouth like that. Instead, as the man left, Joel just smirked, his good hand resting on his bad. Joshua took his seat, sinking into the fine leather, which seemed to massage the old parts of his back, the regions worn down from bartending. He also opened his coat. If Joel saw the gun, he didn't mention it.

"Nice guy," Joshua said. "You two go to Jesus school together?"

"Jesus school, funny." Joel didn't smile. "He's a librarian. We're donating some old Bibles."

"No reason not to," Joshua said. "You only care about the last book."

"Oh, brother Rivers, we live through all of the books. *Revelations* just teaches us how to die."

Joel put on his preacher face, one meant to strike fear in his parishioners, but it just annoyed Joshua.

"I'm glad my messenger was able to convey the urgency of this meeting."

"Your kid's a little wound up. You should take him to a ball game or teach him to drink."

"He's a serious young man, unlike most of the ragtag little alley rats running around here. You understand, of course, our community is drowning under barrels of drink and deviant fornication and it is giving our youth a wicked education."

Joshua let his hands fall to his lap. They were getting to it.

"Can we cut short the sermon?" Joshua said. "How much is this going to cost me?"

Joel threw up his hands in mock outrage, acting dismayed over the end of their double speak. "I'm a man of God. The church seeks offerings, not extortion. I think ten percent should satisfy my parishioners. Don't frown. Think of it as doing some good works for the neighborhood."

Next week a man with a gun would come to his door with an envelope. When he cleared the till that would equal ten percent.

"I'll think on it."

"You shouldn't do too much of that. Thinking's always been bad for your family."

"Look," Joshua said. "The truth is that things are tight right now. I've got a baby on the way and I need a few months to get caught up with—"

"Even the meek have a dollar to share for the funding of our Lord's army. You'll find more than a dollar, I'm sure."

Joshua got up while Joel shoved a pencil beneath his cast, scratching.

"How's the thumb?" Joshua said.

"You can't talk sense with that Mexican." From his desk drawer Joel pulled out an odd-looking photograph and then held it to his lamp. "You ever see one of these?"

Joshua hadn't.

"Doctors call it an X-ray," Joel said. "Takes a photograph underneath the skin."

"What's it tell you?"

"That my thumb is broke. Ten bucks for what I already knew."

"Why were you looking for Olive anyways?"

"I wasn't." Joel looked up. "She was looking for me."

CHAPTER NINE

Joshua should have gone back for the dinner rush but instead wandered over to an old sailor's bar that looked out at the water. It was the type of joint that called itself an oyster house but there hadn't been oysters in the Crabbe for decades, so people ate stale crackers to make the rum go down easier. The bar was nothing more than a lean-to sagging against the edge of the pier, which itself had crumbled at the tip from a storm a few years back. For the first hour, Joshua drank quick and alone, taking the rum and water in long gulps. Nearby a pair of long-shoremen played Blind Man's Bluff, while the bartender swatted cockroaches with an old boot, crying out "Brutus!" when he got one. Joshua had been here once before, with Olive, back when he'd first returned to town. It had been her suggestion. She'd refused to go into the Swill, saying it just didn't have the right feel with their grandmother dead. She'd preferred this dive because she liked to watch the ships coming and going.

"I wouldn't mind getting on one of those boats someday," she'd said. "Finally saying the hell to this town."

"I've been on one of them. You're not missing much."

"Different times, big brother. From what I hear, a girl like me could make a real mark in Berlin."

They had spent that afternoon in the past, talking of their grandmother and Rafael and all the old times at the Swill because they were still feeling each other out, trying to get a sense of one another as adults. He had been gone so long—leaving when she was still a little girl—that he didn't know what kind of woman she'd become. Years later, he realized he still didn't know his sister well enough to guess what she was up to.

When the sun was finally down, a trio of men fell loudly into the bar and latched their eyes upon Joshua like he was their missing brother. Joshua tensed, took down the rest of his drink, and got up to leave, but was too slow and he already had a fresh rum in front of him.

"Stay," said the biggest of the three. He had an anchor tattoo on his neck alongside a charred ear lobe. The other two men seemed to have no other purpose than to laugh at whatever the big one said.

"Got to go to work," Joshua said.

"Ah, work, who needs it?" the big man said. He quickly introduced himself as Otis and he and his two friends were having a reunion. They'd served together on the *Wyoming* hunting U-boats, during the last half of 1918. Otis went on for a while, talking about the action they saw, the Germans they'd drowned. It was the best year of his life.

"Did you fight?" Otis said.

Joshua took the rest of his drink and left a nickel on the table. "No, I'm Canadian."

"They fought as well."

"Flat feet."

CHAPTER TEN

That night a spring rain swept across the road like a right cross. Men, making their way home, hid under newspapers, the ink running down their fingers. The storefronts were shuttered leaving only a feeble melody drifting from Swampy Joyce's tavern. Across the street a pair of old Irish women shared an umbrella, staring at him while clutching their rosaries. To Joshua, Smythe Street looked wrong, as if someone had painted its portrait and forgotten the nose. Even in a blizzard, there was usually someone making noise, be it singing a ballad, starting a brawl, or just plain weeping. Yet the Swill was asleep with just a faint light dribbling from her windows. Joshua shook off under the awning and pulled the door. Locked.

He reached for his key and his gun, a long breath followed by turning the lock and pushing open the door into weak light; down the stairs—quick, two at a time—no sense going slow and quiet when they know you're coming; eyes moving, always moving, the air strung together in waves of blue; on the fourth step, a memory returned, a woman with bright red hair clutching a church's doorframe—he stepped over her to strip away every last offering; back in the bar, halfway down the stairs, the smell of booze, like the tavern he busted up near the Marne; on the landing he raised his gun.

No one cared.

Lily sat with a flank steak pressed to her eye, Miss Amand doing the pressing. Behind them some of the cheaper stock was shattered beside the busted chair that did the swinging. By the kitchen, the Canadian Club lay broken. He started for Lily until Miss Amand flicked her eyes toward little Willie Vanderhock and his cousin sitting on the floor, aching and bloodied. Beside them was Olive wearing the same dress as two nights earlier, while her pistol was leveled at Willie's gut.

"Where've you been?" Lily's right eye was swelling.

He pointed at Willie and started connecting the boy to the broken glass and the bruise on Lily's face. He closed his fists, felt his head fog.

"Met with his father," Joshua said.

"That was hours ago."

With his cracking, pubescent voice, Willie said, "You're in trouble now, aren't you?"

Olive swung her pistol into Willie's face. The boy yelped, pup-like, broken teeth tumbling red down his preacher collar.

"Be a good boy now and raise your hand before you speak," Olive said.

The barroom wobbled. The electric light streaked. Joshua crouched before the boy, steadying against a chair and felt a rush of pain in his left arm like he'd caught a bullet but it just as quickly vanished.

"Did your father send you?" Joshua said. "Answer me."

"No. He don't know we're here. Taking initiative, you see."

"Probably not a good idea," Olive said. She pressed the gun against the boy's cock, winked. Willie dug into the wood, trembling. "When I came around they'd already done a number on the booze and your wife's eye. So I got little Carrie Nation here to reconsider his tact. Might have gotten a bit rough with them."

"You nearly beat them to death, you crazy. . ." Lily's voice trailed off.

Olive moved to the piano bench and casually pet Orla. "You're a good girl," she said to Orla. "I'm starting to like you as much as the old one."

"Are you having fun?" Lily asked.

"You're welcome," Olive said. "Was no trouble at all saving your skin."

It all seemed like a picture show to Joshua, like he was a witness to another family's bad day. He couldn't find his place in the bar, couldn't get his head straight enough to be present. The dizziness came and went and returned again, a dizziness he'd felt a long time ago, usually when there was blood covering his uniform.

Willie began to pull himself up against the wall, while the other boy remained on the ground, fetal and whimpering. Whatever Olive had done stuck with Willie's cousin. Willie was braver, or dumber. It was the sort of bravado that played well in the neighborhood. We've all got to act so tough, Joshua thought. It was exhausting.

But Willie was younger and hadn't seen that many dead men. He was trying to make his name, just like his dad. "My father's going to kill all of you when he hears about this."

Olive lit a cigarette, pointed it at Willie. "Kid, why do you think he'll hear about this at all?"

But Willie wasn't understanding her. He set his face right up against Olive's, trading air.

"You won't kill me," he said.

Sighing, Joshua got to his feet. "She meant cut your tongue out, kid."

"I did," Olive said. "I really did."

Chapter Ten

Lily palmed her mouth.

Cutting out his tongue was just the start: a bag over the boy's head, knock him cold with the butt of a pistol, drive him out to the Sound and weigh him down with bricks. Take that tongue and mail it to his father. It's what *men* did in the Bonny. And Joshua waited for the violence inside of him to make its decision, but it didn't come. So he faked it. He grabbed Willie's jaw, squeezing until the boy squealed, until the tongue came out, small and pink. The boy's face no more than pimples and blood.

"Please, Rivers," Lily said. "You're scaring me."

Joshua held fast to Willie's jaw, felt the eyes of women. He *should* do it, he understood.

"Tell your father, tell him there isn't any call to rush me. Tell him my first payment is letting you keep your tongue. Tell him I'm not sure there'll be a second. Can you remember all that?"

"Joshua," Olive said. "You can't—"

"Let them go," Joshua said. "He's been warned."

Lily rushed up the back stairs. There'd be a long, pained silence for days, he knew.

Meanwhile, Olive crouched and grabbed Willie's hand.

"Tell your father I'll be calling soon," Olive said.

"Okay."

"Not like that. Say 'Yes Miss Rivers.'"

"You—"

Before Willie could finish Olive took his forefinger, brought it to her lips as if she was going to kiss it, before bending it back, all the way to his wrist. The crack echoed through the bar and then there was an emptiness in the air before Willie's cry filled it.

CHAPTER ELEVEN

Miss Amand stood at the bedroom door, reading a book. At the sound of Joshua's steps, she held up her hand—wait—to finish her paragraph. Beside the window, he lit a cigarette, rubbed his temples, the streetlight illuminating his gold-stained fingers before he dropped the cigarette into the remnant pool of an empty vase. Down on the street, Willie slung his arm over the other boy's shoulder for weight. He'd blame Joshua for roughing him up. It was too embarrassing to get rolled by a girl. Vanderhock would have to hit back. Maybe not immediately, but down the line there'd be a reckoning. When the hardback shut, he turned to find Miss Amand with folded hands.

"I gave her something to help her sleep," she said. The baby was fine, Miss Amand told him, but he should find another bed to sleep in.

"She had an awful fright. She's a good girl, but certain customs of our people, well—" She took off her hat, shaking loose silver hair that curled just at the tip. "You did well by her tonight."

"What do you mean? I wasn't here."

"I meant that you did fine not murdering that dull boy. It would have changed her idea of you."

He agreed. He ran his hand along the wall, the yellowing paper decorated in roses hung up fifty years earlier, he was told, in the fashion of the day. A few years back, he'd promised Lily he would strip it and put up something modern, but he'd never found the time.

"I didn't want to hurt him," Joshua said. "I know I'm supposed—well, he's just a kid."

Miss Amand reached into his shirt pocket for a cigarette and after she lit it, the flame seemed to take a few decades off her face.

"I understand," she said. "But remember the Bonny is not a civilized place."

"That's the problem, isn't it?"

"Ah. Civilization has her own devils. They just wear neckties and carry writs."

Olive had already begun sweeping up the broken glass. He lit a fire to get out the booze stench, and then grabbed a second broom. For a while, they worked wordlessly, shoveling up glass, running a mop, knowing what needed to be done to get the joint in order, and then, when their work was finished, she went behind the bar and dunked her hands in the sink, and then said, "We should have sunk that little shit in the Crabbe."

"Lily's not the sinking type of girl."

"She knows what you did in the War."

"That isn't the same as seeing it."

"Fine. But you would have if it wasn't for her?"

"Yeah," he said. "Yeah, of course."

She found the best bottle that hadn't been shattered—a whiskey smuggled up from Tennessee—and then poured three fingers. She slid one glass down to him, the liquor sloshing a bit at the rim, before she raised her own and took a long drink. She'd have made a good barmaid, he thought, if she hadn't become a woman of casual violence. He tried to shake the thought, because, if he conceded to what she'd become—and what she'd become was mysterious and dark and somewhat sick in his mind—he'd never feel comfortable beside her again. They sat together for a couple clock ticks, starting to speak before stopping, and then eventually settling for staring at the kitchen where an iron skillet hung above the stove. He felt the weight of the dead in the room. So did she.

"You know you'll be cursed with a daughter full of hell," she said.

"Just as long as she's not as bad as you."

"I'm just mischievous."

"They don't swear out warrants for that." He rested his head on the bar. The load of the day sunk into his shoulders and he imagined this was what old age felt like. "I should move to California, be done with this town. There's a beach outside of Los Angeles with—"

"Is this your island of magical whales, where all the days are sunny and all the girls are easy?"

"Told you that?"

"Only half a dozen times." She poured a second round. The whiskey was sweet and dangerously smooth. "You're just bored."

"I am bored. And broke. Do you think Grandma was bored? I know she was broke."

"Hell if I know. I wasn't her confessional." Olive took a napkin from behind the bar and began drawing on it. "Remember big brother, hard times are always around the corner and then people will want to visit a joint like this. That's how it works. You're never out of fashion if you're never in fashion."

"You read that somewhere?"

"No, I'm just particularly clever." She paused, wanting to say something but then returned to the napkin.

"What?" he asked.

"Well, I'd rather hang myself than come back here. So I won't talk you out of leaving, which you're pretty good at, leaving. But I hope you do stay, just so I know it's here even if I don't want anything to do with it."

"That's pretty lousy of you."

She held up the napkin. It was a picture of whales fucking. "Yeah, it is."

"Jesus," he said. "What are we doing here? What are we talking about?"

She startled and he realized he was yelling.

"I haven't seen you in a year and you drop by twice this week like some sort of guardian gun moll," he said.

"Guardian gun moll?"

"Stop it," he said. "Don't treat me like a mark. Vanderhock goes around looking for you. I find some Austrian mercenary asking after you, and then you come in and bust up baby Vanderhock and that's all just a coincidence?"

"Well," she said. "I guess I owe you the truth."

"Yeah, you do."

"It's your right as an American."

"Cut it out."

"Okay, okay." She smiled. "Let me start with a question."

"Olive, I swear to God—"

"Okay, okay, listen, just listen. How much would three grand help you out?"

CHAPTER TWELVE

It was midnight when the car stopped in front of the Swill. The storm had left behind a sapphire, moonless sky along with a film of water on the road. Only a couple of the lamps worked on the street, leaving the driver as no more than a silhouette. Joshua got in the back next to Olive, who held a walking stick. She had covered her face in ash, making her look like a bum.

"Lily notice you leave?"

"Still sleeping," he said. "I told Miss Amand I had to take a walk."

"She knows you're lying."

The driver sped off into the dark, which soon gave way to the carnival of Bonny Lane, a spectacle of cheap theaters showing second-rate movies and third-rate plays. Burlesque shows shrouded whorehouses, while, in the basements of dance halls and champagne bars, you could buy opium by the pipe or lay down a bet on a cockfight. Part-time call girls paraded beside simulacrums of mobsters, while the real tough guys, the ones you crossed the street to avoid, stayed off the Lane, preferring joints they owned or 'protected.'

Chapter Twelve

When the car stopped at 21st street, the driver turned and Joshua saw it was Molly, an old friend of Olive's. The pair had been running together for years, pulling badger games and forgeries and second-story jobs all over town. It was clear Olive was the brains behind the partnership, the one whose gait Molly imitated. To Joshua, Molly was nothing but a stringy piece of work with a butterflied nose and the vocabulary of a feral child. He said hello and she told him to go fuck a dog.

"Be nice, you two," Olive said. "Molly's our wheelman tonight."

"What's the job?" Joshua asked.

"Don't you worry your pretty little head about it," Olive said, handing him a pistol and a wool mask, the kind you wore in the Alps, or when you walked into a bank wanting to make a rather large withdrawal. "Now put this on and act tough."

CHAPTER THIRTEEN

He walked past a pair of marble elephants—named *Capital* and *Commerce*—their mouths agape, their trunks raised to the sky, their sheen dulled by car exhaust, and then he took the side stairs, avoiding the footlights aimed at the marble columns, before stopping in a shadow near the entrance to the Port Kydd Public Library. The wind cut through his dark sweater and he reached under his mask to scratch his nose. The street was as quiet as underwater. The storm had swept away the day's smoke and he could see the Little Dipper and Orion, which was about as rare a sight on the Island as an honest cop. He took out the pistol, checked the magazine, and then made sure the chamber was empty just in case he got scared, in case he forgot *when* to fire. A car drove around, passing under one of the bronze signal lights they'd been putting up along the avenue. He shut his eyes, remembered his sergeant screaming "Look, look, look!"

Look where? There was nothing but mud, smoke, and bodies strung along barbed wire.

An hour later the sergeant died scalpless. Joshua had looked then.

Chapter Thirteen

The car pulled up and Olive stepped out and went straight up the library stairs, her cane swinging before her. She dragged her left leg, jerking it up each step with the power of her right.

He crouched behind a column, pistol in his left hand, then his right.

Olive rapped her cane against the iron and glass door, loud enough, Joshua worried, to wake everyone from here to the nearest precinct.

"Help me," she said in an Irish accent. "Let me in boys."

Another car passed, newer, flashier, dragging a train of empty steel food cans. A woman in a wedding veil stuck her head out the back window and screamed at the elephants, "I'm rich!" The car sped off under the canopy of red lights.

Olive slumped against the door, a desperate palm to the glass, fingerprints masked behind ratty opera gloves.

"Please laddie, I'll lay for you."

The lock turned and the opening door let loose a ray of light onto the entranceway, spotlighting Olive, and like a starlet, she fell to her knees.

"Wait 'till you get inside little girl."

Hands reached for Olive's shoulders and her knee swung up into his pants. The man buckled, groaning.

Joshua ran, boots slapping granite, and then threw a haymaker with the dull end of his gun, cracking the guard's nose so loud it seemed to pop Joshua's ears. Blood mushroomed and the guard fell.

"Sorry," Joshua said.

Olive looked at her brother like he was adopted, her gun trained at a second guard behind a desk, his mouth full of salami.

Joshua dragged the bleeding guard by the lapel across the long entryway, over a marble floor that showed a map of Port

Kydd, all the way to the desk. The boy whimpered. "Oh, god. Oh, Jesus. Why'd you got go do that?"

"Stop talking and don't fucking move," Joshua said, using his own Irish accent, which sounded like he was from Bombay. He felt ridiculous but Olive worried their own voices could be used to identify them.

He waved his gun hand at the second guard and told the kid to sit on the floor with his partner. Joshua searched them and found a pair of cheap pistols.

"Five minutes," Olive said, a ski mask now covering her face. "Then leave me."

She went up the stairs, disappearing onto the second floor, while Joshua waited, pockets stocked with firearms, two kids at his feet, one bleeding, the other's pants wet with piss. He thought of Paddy wagons, unforgiving juries, and prison bars but quickly pushed the doubt into the dark part of his gut by imagining a cold, hungry daughter.

"Why you doing this?" the second guard said. He'd covered the wet of his pants with his hat.

"That's a dumb question," Joshua said. "I'll answer when you ask a better one."

"Why are you robbing a library?" the first guard said, his head tilted, blood running in rivulets over his knuckles.

That was a better question, one Olive hadn't answered, just that there was a good score and a buyer lined up who paid cash and kept his secrets secret.

"Trust me," was all she said and he did. After all, it was a simple plan, a good plan. Too much detail, too many complications got people cuffed. For every convoluted job that made the papers, there were two-dozen straightforward smash and grabs that no one—not even the cops—ever heard about.

"Are you going to kill us?" the second guard said. "I got a mama who, who—"

"You two talk too much."

But then they all stopped talking with the approach of slow, heavy steps coming down the stairs. Joshua put his finger to his lips—quiet—and then hoisted the second guard to his feet, collaring him out front, his gun's muzzle propping up the boy's head. Joshua squeezed the grip, his hands damp. The boy's shoulders shivered and his hair smelled like vinegar. Two more steps, thumps like a bass drum before pausing, loafers visible through the railing slats. The guard sniffled. Joshua dug the muzzle into the back of the boy's skull. A match snapped against a striker, followed by a long, smoky exhale, before the man continued his march.

He came down wearing a dark suit and glasses and smoking from a cigarette holder, only pausing, for a moment, to glance back, before continuing. He hummed.

Joshua recognized him—the Librarian from Vanderhock's church.

On the last stair, the Librarian paused, looked straight at Joshua's masked face, and then tapped his cigarette.

"Top of the morning," Joshua said, still playing Irish.

The Librarian fixed his glasses and looked over the boy and Joshua and then the other boy as if they were all strays. No weeping here. This was a cool one.

"To you as well," the Librarian said.

Joshua motioned toward the bench. "Want to take a seat?"

"Seems like a very good idea."

The Librarian looked over the bloodied guard and, when satisfied the kid would live, he sat and returned to his smoking. Joshua pushed the second guard to the floor and then checked his watch. Only two long minutes had passed.

"It will be over soon," the Librarian said.

"What?" Joshua asked.

"You're nervous, which seems appropriate given the consequences should you be arrested. Not only will you face the chair, but your conscience will be tainted by the blood you let."

"They don't give the chair for crippling you a bit."

The Librarian took off his glasses, examined them by the lamp on the desk, and then cleaned them with his tie. "Young man, if you've ever seen Ireland, it was only through a stereoscope."

"Seen France. Should tell you enough."

The Librarian pointed to the floor above. Footsteps.

"Perhaps your partner is more capable with his accent."

Olive ran down the stairs, a cylinder of paper under her arm. She looked at Joshua and then the guards and the Librarian and then again at Joshua.

"Tie them up or knock them out, will you? What the hell's wrong with you?"

"I was correct," the Librarian said. "Her accent is vastly superior."

Joshua raised the pistol to the Librarian's nose like a batter waiting for a pitch.

"Excuse me," the Librarian said. "But perhaps you'd be so kind as to lock us in the coat check? It would be a much more pleasant manner to pass the evening."

Joshua turned to his sister.

"Fine," Olive said. "Hurry up."

Into the cloak closet they went, two scared guards and a librarian without a care. As he shut the door, Joshua caught what he thought was a smile from the Librarian. The world takes all kinds, Joshua figured. He met Olive at the door and they peered through the glass at a street free of cops. They walked out toward the marble elephants, Olive pulling off her mask, face sweat-bright.

"Where's Molly?" Joshua asked.

"She'll be here."

Chapter Thirteen

He reached for his own mask until he saw a shadow that lit a spark in his jaw. On the way to the ground, a figure in blue loomed then howled.

Joshua rolled onto his belly, felt his face on fire. Hands flat on the ground, a voice—imagined—told him to "get up, get up," and he did, only to find two figures struggling, blurred. Then clear.

Olive kneeled over a cop, his nightstick in her hand and she hit him with swift, practiced strokes that sounded like she was beating a sack of flour. She kept going, one after the other, right into his face, blood pouring from a gash on his forehead, from his nose, from his mouth.

"Cut it out," Joshua said.

She kept on and on, only quitting when Molly honked the horn.

CHAPTER FOURTEEN

Down the avenue, lights flicking by like fireflies. Face to the window, jaw jelly. His panting fogged the glass.

Olive reached for his chin and it felt like a landmine going off.

"You'll need some ice but you'll live," she said.

Molly turned into a car barn and shut the engine. Olive leaned into the front seat, unraveling the cylinder over Molly's lap. He listened for sirens.

"My god," Molly said.

"Oh, baby, it was a beautiful sight. My knife slit along the frame and they slipped right out and just look at them. You see 'em? You too Joshua."

"I'm fine."

"I think you'll want to see this one," Olive said.

Her tone sent his eyes over.

There were four paintings in all, the canvases about the length of his arm, each an impressionistic mess of greens and reds and blues but when his eyes made sense of it, he felt a punch to the throat. A riot on Smythe Street; a female nude at his own bedroom window; a street-scene, no, a *Smythe street-scene* with pushcarts brimming with fruit and costume jewelry and secondhand boots and young men on the make and horses trotting past the banks of manure. When Olive stopped on the last painting, she held its pose, and he knew what it was, and who it was: two thieves, running down the street, one carrying a sword and the other a pistol, the Swill looming in the background; two women on the edge of the scene, one on the street under a parasol, the second looking down from her bedroom window; a pair of nuns praying; a preacher on his soapbox; a gang of drunks raising their pistols at the orange sky; and, at the center, a dead body surrounded by hogs, and behind them stands a young Black child.

He felt something fall on his lap and when he looked down today's problems went away—a pile of hundred-dollar bills, as thick as a porterhouse, making love to his thigh.

"Don't know why he gets such a large cut," Molly said. "That's most of our savings."

"Earned it," Olive said, her gaze fixed on *The Passenger Pigeons* like she was memorizing it. "Busted a guy up pretty good."

"Why?" Joshua asked.

"Stop it," Olive said. "You know why."

He fell out of the car, a wad of cash in his boot, and his jaw tolling. A cold wind scattered cigarette butts and funneled newspapers into a whirlwind. The car sped off. He buttoned his coat and made his way down Bonny Lane, past all of the theaters that had come and gone, been burnt and resurrected, thunder cracking off in the distance, lightening flashing out over the Crabbe, the painting etched in his mind, the story of its birth a tale of his people.

PART TWO: THE FIRST PAINTING

CHAPTER FIFTEEN

December 6th, 1873—Port Kydd, USA

A distant thunder drew Nellie Rivers from her easel to the window. She parted the curtains, her fingers stained by old paint, hands peeling from dishes, nails blackened by dirt and ash. Outside, the sunset tinted the coal smoke a kind of mustard. Mud dripped from hog snouts. On the corner, Mrs. O'Reilly, a wet nurse, threw her house slop out the second story window, sending a rainbow of night soil that nearly drenched Lulu Daly. There were no storm clouds, just a shake of sound like an army coming to conquer.

She thought herself crazy, looked down at her pregnant belly, laid the blame on it. "You're the cause of my madness."

But Nellie Rivers was still right of mind. In fact, she was in her prime for a woman in Port Kydd, and especially for one in her neighborhood. She was twenty-two, owned a fairly reputable tavern, had a man who might marry her, and that was about as good as it got.

Down on the street, the Negro shit-shovelers planted their spades between cobblestones and looked west. A pair of nuns, still wearing the dark of Dùn Laoghaire across their eyes, fingered their rosaries. Billy-Bailey Vanderhock, a strange, squat man, preached from his soapbox to a congregation of none. All the ordinary characters. She was disappointed. There hadn't been a spectacle in weeks, nothing worth a clean canvas, but then a flash of movement sent her gaze west.

Something slumped down the road.

At first, she couldn't make sense of it. A giant leashing a dwarf? A constable shackling a child? But as the figures crossed over Lancaster Street, pushing through a crowd of men just off their shift from the brickworks, she saw it was a sailor dragging a Black child. He was being shanghaied out to sea.

The sailor was one of those slouching one-eyed beasts common to its trade, but the boy was a beauty. Maybe eight or nine. Those big eyes! Wide as the Morgan River. And that mouth! If he ever took up cards, he'd be king of this city. Nothing there but strength and a hint of mean. She leaned over the windowsill, only tilting back when Orla trotted over for a scratch on the ass.

"You're a good girl and you make me feel less hysterical."

A cold wind bit her bare arms, so she crossed the room, stepping over a mess of drop cloths and brushes and paint tubes. Against the dresser leaned a drying painting, a streetscape of All Saints' Day, when two fire brigades rumbled with bare chests and flailing chains. She'd sat at the window with her sketchpad, watching it like a play. It was a powerful painting, she thought, maintaining a sense of realism to it, but also heightened and fragmented, giving it motion, punctuating the absurdity of the violence.

From the closet she picked out a dressing gown and then returned to her stool, sitting across from the primed canvas.

"Oh, Orla, will you sit for me? We'll call it *Canine in Repose*."

But Orla had vanished. The bedroom door was shut, the closet empty, so Nellie peaked under the bed where the mutt hid, trembling.

Chapter Fifteen

"Visions of cats again?"

The floor shivered. The air smelled rancid. The sun had gone out, dark as midnight at ten in the morning. A moment passed before the thunder was on them, a great tempest if Nellie had ever heard one. Orla howled.

Nellie found a cigar and then shimmied onto the windowsill, struck a match, when she saw *it* approaching from the west—

A great wave of bronze swallowing the sky.

She dropped her cigar and mouthed the name of God.

It was like no storm she'd ever seen, textured and woven with colors in layers, as if Manet had painted the *Book of Revelations*. There was a sort of flatness to the horizon, an erasing of the curvature of the Earth, the western sky devoured under an invasion of color. She gripped the sill, thought of her dead mother, and prayed.

On the street, the shit-shovelers raised their spades like swords and the nuns bowed their heads and the sailor cropped the boy. Little Billy-Bailey stood tip-toed, calling out, "Let the heathens burn!" An old woman in a green dress stopped beside Billy-Bailey and looked to the sky. Over by Johnny Doyle's suicide palace, smiths and masons and lay-abouts spilled onto the street, celebrating St. Nicholas' Feast, drunk on spiked lightening to the last.

Nellie shut her eyes. "Our father, who art in heaven, hallowed—"

Yet, before she could finish the verse, her fear fell away under the power of wonder. She found another cigar and returned to the windowsill to smoke it proper. After all, this was a sort of miracle, a way to mark time and she'd have to be dragged off the sill by the hand of God himself.

Did the Bonny think the same? Did the Bonny quiet her mind in awe? Of course not. The Bonny did what the Bonny did when encountering the majestic.

Chapter Fifteen

She greeted her with violence.

One of Doyle's drunks fired off a single shot.

A beat of silence followed before something crashed to the ground. They all leaned in for a look.

A bird. Slate gray with a bronze belly.

His cronies followed with a crescendo of gunfire that sent a bloody, feathered rain upon Smythe Street. Birds crashed onto the cobblestone, painting the street red. One fell across Nellie's leg, smearing blood along her calf. She picked it up. A passenger pigeon. A bad omen most said. They had come before and brought dark magic. In 1689, a dozen babies had been born with nine toes. In 1734, a poor crop led to famine. And the last time, in 1861, there were riots and cholera. But on St. Nicholas' Day in 1873, no one remembered the past, including Nellie. She thought them beautiful and their slaughter a sin. She couldn't abide it any longer.

"Cut that goddamn nonsense out you fucking bastards," Nellie yelled. "They ain't doin' you no damned harm."

She turned to the sailor cropping the boy and the sailor felt her stare, their eyes meeting, before his mouth twisted into a frightening grin, like a man possessed, and half his skull fell away, his brains seeping down his shoulder to the street, before he dropped. A stray bullet had fallen back to Earth.

"Oh my god," she said.

The little Black boy stood above him, stunned.

Below her windowsill, a man in a fine suit and a woman covered by a camisole, stepped onto the street. Nellie wanted to shout at them to take cover, but then, out to the east, she saw two men running toward the gunfire, ducking avian cannonballs, running like the town was sinking back into the Crabbe. She thought they were madmen, escapees from Flywell's asylum before recognizing them. The pale one, her lover, slipped on a bird and then tumbled to the ground. The brown one, the most beautiful man she'd ever seen, picked up his friend. She hoped they'd come to end this bird massacre, to show Doyle's drunks true manliness, but she should have known better. Three men in dark suits stepped out from the livery. They raised their rifles.

And then Nellie turned away.

That's how she remembered it.

That's the story she told for the next fifty years.

She turned away and saw nothing thereafter. The moment petrified. The story that followed erased from her private history.

She went to her stool and sat before her canvas. She had the image in her head, knew the *truth*.

CHAPTER SIXTEEN

<u>October 23, 1929—Port Kydd, USA</u>

Thunder cracked in the mid-morning, so loud Joshua nearly missed the phone's ring. He picked it up, while eying the vat of onion soup simmering on the stove, a feast that cost him next to nothing.

"Swill."

"Mr. Rivers." It was a young woman's voice. "My name is Miss Charlene Crane, head secretary for Mr. Jasper Smythe, of Smythe Holdings. I am calling—"

"That seems like a nice gig."

"Well, um, yes, I am calling because Mr. Smythe would like for you to meet him at the Port Kydd Library this afternoon. He has a few questions he would like for you to answer."

"The library?"

"Yes, it's the rather large building with all of the books. Does two o'clock fit on your calendar?"

Joshua grabbed a pad and pen, and then, after he wrote down the name and time, he reached for a glass, but it slipped and shattered on the floor. He bent down to pick up the shards, a jagged edge nicking his finger.

Chapter Sixteen

"Goddammit."

"Excuse me, Mr. Rivers?"

"Sorry. What does he want to ask me about in this place with all the books?"

"Mr. Rivers." She took a long breath. "I haven't the faintest idea why he would wish to speak to someone like you."

After he hung up, Joshua glanced at the floor, where, below the broken glass, in the dugout, sat the money from Olive's job. Six months later and it was still doing him no good. Once in a while, he took a little out, stuck it in the till, and acted like he'd had a good night, but for the most part it stayed put because Lily didn't know about it. So when she'd gone out earlier with her mother to look for a bassinet, she'd planned on buying used, threadbare. The lie ate at him, sometimes keeping him from looking her in the eye, but he'd sooner turn the Swill into a teahouse than confess to the library job. Now Smythe was calling for God knew what reason. He hadn't ever come across a Smythe in person, never entered their rarified circle, though he'd heard enough stories to know they meant him no good. He took a drink straight from the bottle, looked at the dog asleep beneath the piano bench, and calmed himself. Play dumb. That's what everyone expected. He dug through the junk box under the invoices, pulling out bills, playing cards, and forgotten wallets, before coming up with an old number for Olive, but when the operator said the line was out of use, he took his umbrella and gun over to Pinebox Square to look for her.

By the time he reached Maiden Street the rain had let up, leaving the gutters full of apple cores, cigarette butts, and spent bandages. Most of the speaks wouldn't open until sundown, yet the ones serving had their doors open wide, smoke pouring out, Volstead be damned. Even the light seemed dirtier. The neighborhood had been built on top of an old reservoir and when it rained the street flooded ankle deep, resurrecting the stench of fossilized fish, while the sidewalk rolled in slopes and divots and some buildings threatened to sink right back into the caverns below. If you were born in Pinebox Square, you spent your whole life trying to get out and if you didn't get out, you were as good as soul dead. Those left behind included nickel and dime crooks, girls in suits and boys in dresses, and all those types catering to needs that couldn't be met through the Sears catalog.

The first bar he stepped into, a dive called the Dead Pelt, stunk of lye though it didn't look to Joshua like it had seen a mop since the War. A couple napped on the floor beside a mud pit used for dog fighting. Neither had shoes on, their feet soot-black, a torn slip shrouding their faces. Over by the bathroom door, there was a baby sharing a blanket with a wiener dog. Then, after the flush of the toilet, out stepped the barmaid, a real bruiser. After he told her who he was looking for, she told him to eat it. The next place, the next barmaid, echoed the first. But at the third tavern, a hole called Mags' Hangout, he got lucky. The bar was no more than a single green door off an alley, bracketed by a hatter and a stonemason who specialized in grave markers. Once inside, he got slugged in the nose by the scent of raw whiskey being distilled out back, the kind of booze that fortunately blinded you first, so you couldn't see the mess you made in your pants. A single oil lamp burned by the back door. After his eyes adjusted to the dark, he saw that there was no bar, just a handful of tables surrounding a washtub full of unlabeled liquor bottles. Two young men hunched over a bowl of salted fish, eating with their hands. An older woman, wearing a headscarf and muumuu, scraped the wax off an opium pipe with a switchblade, while a stringy blonde in a ratty yellow dress hummed at the window, even though the shades were down. She was pretty, Joshua thought, if you didn't mind them hopped-up and underage. The barmaid was taunting the rat cages, warming up the rodents for the night's fight. Her hair was wrapped in a red bandana and she wore nothing but a bra under her overalls. After she saw him, she wiped her hands with a rag and then pulled out a pair of brass knuckles. They looked like a hand-me-down.

He asked after Olive.

"Know her, sure. Now you, you I never heard of."

"I'm her brother. I run the Swill over in the Bonny."

"Don't like posh places." She spit snuff at one of the rats. "Something funny?"

There was but given her set-up, she wouldn't think so. She kept wearing those brass knuckles but with her free hand, she reached into her pocket and pulled out a pair of bifocals and put them on.

"See you look a little like her. Not much but a little."

"Different fathers."

"Isn't that always the story?"

"She come around here lately?"

"Can't remember."

He'd left his wallet at home, figuring flashing any leather would get him rolled but a couple of bills in his pocket was no loss. He handed her a five and she checked its authenticity near the lamplight.

"Comes in once in a while," she said. "When we got a good fight."

"Didn't know she went for rats."

"Nah. Animals make her sad. Too sweet, that girl. Gonna get her dead someday. But she likes when the girls fight, the big girls. Friday nights. Yeah, you'll find her on Friday nights."

It was Monday.

"If you see her, tell her I need to talk," Joshua said.

"If I tell her anything."

He lowered the brim of his hat, looking tough. "So that's what five bucks buys me?"

Chapter Sixteen

Mags folded the five-dollar bill then held it to the light—it was in the shape of a cock and balls—before pushing it down her bra head first. "Five lets you walk out of here without holes in your gut. That's the market these days."

He stepped out into the sunlight, taking a moment to steady himself. He lit a cigarette, put the pack back in his coat, and looked up to find that stringy blonde standing in front of him. Her patchy skin was a bit jaundiced, but there were no folds under her eyes, no tree rings along her forehead. Coquettishly, she pointed at his coat and he gave her a cigarette.

"I know Olive. Know her real good. We're close, like sisters. Yep."

"Can you tell her that I'm looking for her?"

"I can."

"But—"

"Ten bucks."

"I'll give you three."

"But you gave Mags five."

"Price went down now that Mags said she'd talk to Olive."

The girl slumped and turned away, puffing on her cigarette but not really inhaling. He started moving down the alley and she rushed up beside him.

"Give me ten and I'll talk to Olive."

"It's three."

"How 'bout I give you a suck and talk to Olive. That worth ten, Mister?"

"Jesus." Joshua looked the girl over again. If this was what having a daughter was like, he prayed for a son. "How old are you?"

"Be fifteen come April."

He handed her a five.

"That ain't worth a suck, Mister."

"Go get yourself a plate of real food and tell Olive to come see me."

Afterward he tried a few more taverns, dropped a few more bills, but nothing came of it except some kind salutations like "eat it" or "beat off" or "I'm going to kill you." He bought a bottle at a corner joint, stuck it in his pocket to warm her and then took a few slugs on his walk back home. It was turning into a nice enough day, pleasant even, for fall. The trees had ripened into oranges and reds and even the coal stink had an autumn flavor to it. He wondered how you dressed a child for winter. He thought they should sequester the baby and Lily until spring, but she'd have none of it. "The baby needs fresh air," Lily said. And where would you find fresh air in this goddamn town? He was thinking on this when he reached the Swill and found a guy around 40 years old, wearing a trench coat and carrying a nice camera, one Lily might like. He held it in front of a good-looking face, the kind you wouldn't mind taking a swing at after a few morning drinks.

"Help you?" Joshua said.

The photographer looked him over, made up his mind and then shook his head, no. He pointed the camera at the third-story window—Joshua's bedroom window—and snapped a picture. Joshua looked up, expecting Lily naked at the window, but there was nothing but curtain.

"You got a problem?" Joshua asked.

"Problem? What do you mean?" His voice was gruff and sounded like it came from somewhere else.

"You want to buy the building or something?"

"No. Just like old buildings."

"That's my bedroom window."

"Your bedroom? Hmm."

He lowered his camera and gave Joshua an up and down, appraising him like a car for sale. "Bigger than I thought you'd be. Less delicate. Thought she liked delicate."

The photographer reached into his pocket and Joshua tensed, before the man pulled out a bottle in a brown paper bag and took a slug. He offered it to Joshua.

"No."

"Lily Stern live here?"

"Sure."

"You're the husband?"

"Right."

"Okay. No need to be tough. Figured as much. We're old friends, me and Lily."

He pulled out a pack of cigarettes from his other coat pocket, offered one to Joshua, who saw they were Gauloises. They cost three times more than Lucky Strikes and were almost impossible to find in America.

"How?"

"Know a queer little Canadian in town. He got me some."

"Roche."

"That's the one. Reason I'm dropping by really. Said my father was passing through."

"Thought you were here for Lily?"

"Coincidence," the man said. "Knew Lily a few years back, you know, before you, but really I'm here for my father."

"Haven't seen him."

"This is the type of place he'd drink. Old, off the beaten path, not a lot of customers I'm figuring, no offense meant."

"Doesn't ring a bell."

"How would you know? Haven't even said what he looks like yet."

"I know."

"So that's how it is?"

Chapter Sixteen

The photographer took a long drag from the cigarette and then dropped it on the ground, only half-smoked, before mashing it out. Like a rich asshole. "I'd ask you to tell her Neal stopped by but I'm guessing it'll slip your mind."

"She's pregnant. Really pregnant."

"Tends to be that way. You are or you aren't."

The man looked over the Swill one last time before walking away.

Downstairs, Lily stood over the soup, stirring. She wore men's combat boots, bought from the surplus store, two sizes bigger than her usual because her feet had swollen over the summer and hadn't gone back to normal with the autumn. She tipped back on her heels, a hand braced on her hip, her belly expansive and frightening. When he stepped in and kissed her on the cheek, she didn't bother smiling.

"Where were you?"

"Took a walk."

"With your gun?"

He tasted the soup, added some salt, while she held up a piece of paper with Jasper Smythe's name on it.

"Anything you want to tell me that you weren't planning on telling me?"

"He just wants to chat about something," Joshua said. "Didn't say what."

He added some pepper to the soup along with a slug of wine. The photographer was still bothering him. It seemed strange that on the day Jasper called, a stranger showed up asking after his wife with her maiden name. Lily came up behind him and asked again, this time smacking him with a ladle.

"What are you keeping from me?"

"Smythe's mother," Joshua said, "knew my grandmother a little."

Chapter Sixteen

She looked over him until it made him angry. He didn't like her accusing him of lying even if he was.

"That's mysterious enough," Lily said. "Well, let's go together. I could use the adventure."

He lowered the soup to a simmer and then pulled out a loaf of bread to slice. It was hard, maybe three days old. There was only a bit of blue on it, though.

"Sounds fun," he said.

CHAPTER SEVENTEEN

They stopped at the bottom of the library's stairs and Joshua casually looked around for bloodstains, but of course those washed away months ago. In March, when it all happened, the papers had mentioned the cop, who'd recovered, and the stolen paintings, which hadn't, but it had all quickly faded from public memory, though, he suspected, not Lily's. At the time, she hadn't even known his grandmother was a painter. It just never came up, he told her when she read the story—and eyed his bruised jaw—but today it would be at the center of everything.

At the edge of the stairs, Lily stuck her hand into one of the marble elephant's mouths while he snapped a picture.

"Looks like I'm your Watson today," she said.

"My what?"

"You know, your sidekick, your Sancho Panza. I'm fat enough. Every detective needs a loyal assistant."

"I'm no detective."

"You used to be a Pinkerton."

He led her up the stairs past mothers and children unwinding with cheese sandwiches and cream sodas.

"It's not like that," he said. "There isn't much brainwork with the Pinkertons. Mostly I chased bums out of banks."

They stepped inside to marble walls and marble cornices and poor Russians learning English. He spied a pair of Pinkerton-types, who, Joshua figured, couldn't read an alphabet book if you'd spotted them A through Y.

"When I was a little girl my father took me here every Friday after school," Lily said. "Have you ever been here?"

He didn't have a chance to lie before the Pinkertons came over and led them upstairs to the main reading room where they stopped beside a pair of school kids working on their long division. There were rows of tables with brass lamps lighting up books read by college students in letterman sweaters and immigrants in skullcaps. Along the wall a mural depicted the founding of Port Kydd with Dutch explorers handing baskets of blankets and food to Indians.

Lily pointed across the room at a man with a gray moustache and a double-breasted suit. "Is that him?"

"No," the smaller Pinkerton said. "Over there."

"You're kidding?" Lily said.

"Rich people," the bigger Pinkerton said, "don't make no goddamn sense to me."

He was right. For a man nearly as wealthy as Ford, Jasper Smythe wasn't whom they were expecting. At a glance he came across as someone twenty years out of time, a remnant of the world before the War, with his derby, brown wool jacket, and narrow trousers. All of it was ill-fitting and sloppy, like he hadn't bothered to buy new clothes since his mother stopped dressing him. He was about fifty with a carpet of whiskers along his jaw that made him look like he worked with his hands, though Joshua doubted he could swing a hammer if you handed it to him handle first. He stood amongst a cohort of other moneyed types while lecturing to them like Mother Jones on the topic of poverty in Port Kydd, something Joshua figured he knew a damn thing about. It was all part of his mayoral campaign.

"Gentlemen," Jasper began, "what the poor need is a strong hand to herd them out of their indolence. But it is not hopeless. Look at the wonders Italy's leader has enacted in the heart of the beast."

Lily fiddled with her Leica. It was an older, cheaper camera than the one her "old friend" had been carrying earlier. The man's smirk still bothered Joshua, like he knew something about his wife that Joshua didn't.

"What do you think?"

"Looks like just a jackass with a funny hat," Lily said. "What do you know of him?"

"Not much."

Joshua explained that Jasper had inherited his family fortune after his older brother died of typhoid. In a way, he wasn't meant to be king and it made him an odd duck for the work. Like Joshua, Jasper had wandered the country, trying on new hats, rambling from one hobby to the next, operating a railroad, going out with Lillian Gish, and trying to fly across the country before running out of gas over St. Louis.

"There are better places to crash," Lily said.

"No kidding. There's a girl there who put a curse on me."

"Oh, that's small potatoes. I once sacrificed a chicken because a man didn't like a picture I'd taken of him."

"I like all of your pictures."

"For the sake of American chickens, you'd better."

When Jasper finished his speech, one of the Pinkertons pointed at the Riverses and Jasper came over, his hand outstretched and Joshua was about to take it when he saw a familiar man flanking him, one he hadn't seen in six months, not since he'd stopped by the Swill looking for Olive.

"Mr. and Mrs. Rivers," Jasper said. "I am pleased you've come. And this is Mr. Hess. He works on my campaign."

"We've met," Joshua said.

Jasper turned to Hess.

"Mister Rivers and I had a brief conversation in the spring over the matter involving his sister," Hess said, whose English, Joshua noted, had improved.

"Oh, yes," Jasper said. He took off his hat, revealing tightly waxed hair like you'd see on a doll, and then walked away.

"After you," Hess said.

Jasper gave a tour of the library's collection, which included a Gutenberg Bible, a first folio of Shakespeare, and an edition of Galileo's *The Starry Messenger* in the original Latin, all pieces worth a hell of a lot more than an Eleanor Rivers. Although Jasper knew his stuff, Joshua got the feeling he didn't care much for it, sort of like a jailbird showing you the rocks he's busted. He guided them into a narrow hall that led into an oval room with a bright blue gleam from the skylight, a few shelves of books locked behind glass, and a marble bench dead center.

"Now over in this wing you'll find some of the rarest books in the library's collection, early editions of Dante, Milton, and Marlowe, though if you can understand any of it, you're a better man than me," he said. "And up here, you once were able to view the works of your grandmother."

Four empty, gold-gilded frames hung from the wall.

"The thief cut out the pictures, interesting," Lily said.

"You're a master of observation," Jasper said.

Joshua felt an old rage return, but he told himself that it was just another rich asshole. Nothing more.

"Thanks for the tour but what's this got to do with me?" Joshua said. "My grandmother sold those pictures before I was born."

Chapter Seventeen

"My mother always said you were a naturally suspicious people. It's in the blood, I suspect, like the Royal Disease," Jasper said.

Lily smiled like when someone complained about the food at the Swill.

"Just like that," she said.

Jasper led them down a spiral staircase into the bowels of the library, where they passed into a locked cage housing old, forgotten books. Joshua kept his hands by Lily and his eyes on Hess. The Austrian walked a step ahead, occasionally glancing back, as if he was making sure his dog was still leashed. Jasper opened a door and inside there was a long counter stacked with magnifying glasses, lamps, and tweezers manned by two men in lab coats hunched over a very old-looking canvas. Alongside them stood the fat man from the night of the robbery. Joshua stopped in the doorway and looked right into the Librarian's eyes and thought about what his own arrest would do to his family. But nothing happened. If the Librarian recognized him, he didn't say anything. Meanwhile, Jasper had gone over to the painting, and then, like a magician, flung his arm out as if he'd just materialized a bunny from a top hat.

"May I present *The Passenger Pigeons* by Eleanor Rivers," Jasper said.

He wasn't lying. It was right there, stretched out and under a lamp, looking exactly like the painting Joshua had seen in the car with Olive, with the same dark edges and familiar characters.

"It's like Renoir," Lily said.

"It's like Renoir ten years before Renoir became Renoir," the Librarian said.

Meanwhile, Hess seemed to search Joshua's face for a reaction. Joshua gave him nothing but confusion.

"Where'd you find it?" Lily asked.

"Someone called the cops and told them to check the home of Harlan Law, the famed architect," the Librarian said. "I'm Horace Raab, by the way, Mr. and Mrs. Rivers."

Raab didn't mention meeting Joshua at Vanderhock's church six months back. Maybe he'd forgotten, Joshua thought, but it didn't seem likely.

"Our chief curator," Jasper said. "He is authenticating it now with all of his, I don't know, pseudo-science voodoo, but to my eye, I'll testify to its bona fide-ede-ness."

Lily nodded. Polite. "I'm sure, but what's your stake in this? The papers gave the impression that the library owned these paintings."

"I own them," Jasper said, sneering like a child asked to share. "They simply borrow."

Jasper turned to Joshua. "I'm surprised you didn't know that. Your sister certainly did."

They were getting to it, Joshua knew. He asked what Jasper meant by that.

"Just that your sister and I had a conversation about the paintings one afternoon and then a few weeks later they disappeared."

"Huh."

"What?" Jasper asked.

"Just said, 'huh.' You could have brought me down here six months ago, but you didn't," Joshua said. "Now one just appears out of thin air and suddenly you want to see me. Find that funny is all."

"I haven't any idea what you're implying."

He knew exactly what Joshua was implying.

"Do you know where she is?" Jasper asked. "I'd like to send her a message."

"I haven't heard from Olive in over a year."

"Mr. Rivers, these are crucial times in my campaign. The heart of the city is at stake and I can't have someone like your sister—"

"What's she like?" Joshua said.

"You know exactly what she is."

"Can't help you, pal. Like I said, haven't seen her, could be dead for all I know."

"Well," Jasper said, "if she manages to resurrect herself, tell her simply that like buildings, women and children burn under flame. Do you understand me Mr. Rivers or should I spell it out for you?"

Joshua walked stiffly to the painting, his left leg dragging behind his right, an old war wound long forgotten. He wanted another look at *The Passenger Pigeons*. When he first saw it in the car, he thought it chaotic, just one of those messes only rich people loved. Whatever he'd known of his grandmother was invisible on the canvas to him. The hard woman who raised him, the one who valued a day's work, who went to mass every Sunday, who mourned her dead daughter with prayer candles, couldn't be the same who'd idled away days on something like this. Though he knew it was her work, like he knew the Earth was round, the Nellie Rivers he remembered couldn't be reconciled with *this* Eleanor Rivers. He gripped the table, took a long breath to calm the kicking in his chest, and leaned closer, to see the brushstrokes, to find her hand, but all he felt was a creeping numbness. That surprised him. He always imagined this painting would do something to his soul and reveal a truth about his grandmother and his family and especially the Bonny, that it would help him understand whether he lived among the good or the evil. It didn't. He shut his eyes, felt dizzy.

Like buildings, women and children burn under flame.

He knew that he'd kill Hess first, a kick to the kneecap to drop him, and then come around back and snap his neck. From there, he'd take Hess' gun and finish the rest of them, the two technicians, the fat librarian, and, of course, Jasper himself. The room was deep in the basement, insulated from the rest of the library. No one would hear the shots. By the time they found the bodies, he'd be safely heading west as fast as a stolen car could take him. Only Lily would carry the memory but she'd be alive, as would their child. As he considered this, as he wondered how she'd look at him afterward, he noticed his hands had stopped shaking.

"I didn't think you had a sense of humor," Joshua said, standing tall. "Burning, ha. You should know that I'm not some boarding school princess."

"Are you threatening me?" Jasper said.

"This is all a little fraught, don't we think, over a painting," Raab, the librarian, said. "Now let cooler heads prevail."

"Threatening a man's family," Joshua began. "As a joke. I'm going to take it as a joke. Otherwise, you won't like where this goes."

"Mr. Rivers, please," said Raab.

Jasper laid his hand on Hess' shoulder. The mercenary glanced at the hand and Jasper removed it. "Remember Mr. Rivers," Jasper said. "These stories between our families always end the same way."

Lily started Joshua toward the door, her fingers digging into his forearm. He was glad, he realized, that he brought her along. If she'd been at home, maybe he would have done something. At the door, she turned to the room.

"Thank you for the tour," Lily said. She aimed her camera at Hess and fired. "I do weddings, portraits, and funerals."

By the time they got outside, the wind remembered it was October and Joshua wrapped his coat around Lily while leaves rained from the trees. They pushed through the crowds of bankers in pinstriped suits and secretaries in smart sweaters, hoping to disappear into the anonymity of the uptown rush.

"Why'd you lie to him, about Olive? You saw her six months ago."

"He doesn't need to know that."

CHAPTER EIGHTEEN

They walked east through Knight City Park, where walnuts, elms, and dogwoods surrounded the Great Pond, which, despite the city's best efforts, stunk of dead fish and had a vaguely copper color on the surface. Lily took Joshua's hand and led him down a gravel path past the merry-go-round and a hotdog stand. The wind blew and he brushed a strand of hair from her eyes. Around the park, the city's captains of industry kept their families in palatial townhomes with large iron gates at the entrance to each street. It was how the town worked. As Port Kydd grew, the rich kept moving north to escape the rabble. You couldn't walk through here without your downtown stink waking up every cop in the precinct. But this was as far as the rich could go, bumping right up against Herhalling, the old Black neighborhood, settled by freedmen during Reconstruction. Nearby a pair of women, a mother and grandmother, strolled a child, an heir to a fortune so vast Joshua's own coming daughter could work for a thousand years and never catch up.

As they came out of the park and crossed under the train tracks, Lily mentioned that this whole section was farmland back when the Swill was built, and even when his grandmother was a girl during the Civil War, there'd only been a few scattered farms. Now, nothing of the wild remained.

"Your grandmother was really something," Lily said. "The brushwork was magnificent. And her vision of all those figures moving in tandem centered around the Negro boy was stunning. The two men running—"

"Rafael and Jude. Might as well call them by name."

"Jude's your grandfather, right?"

Joshua nodded.

They crossed over a dirt knoll and went up to the edge of the stone levee and looked out at the dark of the Crabbe. Joshua crossed his arms, while Lily snapped a picture of a skiff motoring toward Flywell Island. From the shore, Joshua could see the orphanage and asylum and prison. A half a dozen Riverses had been jailed there over the past hundred and fifty years. Probably had a reserved cell, he thought.

"I've always been jealous of painters," Lily said. "We both trade in images, but I'm a slave to this machine. Your grandmother did it through the mind's eye. I could sense the sadness in it, the grief for how broken the city was, especially, well, with what happened that day. I can kind of see why Olive stole them."

She kept her eyes toward the water, while seagulls circled overhead. They reminded Joshua of the passenger pigeons, how millions had swarmed the sky when his grandmother was a girl, how the birds went extinct right before the last war. That painting was from another world, right before the Bonny changed forever. It might as well have been a portrait of Julius Caesar for all the good it did him.

"I've never been threatened," she said, hesitating. "But I know you'll get us out of this."

He threw a stone into the Crabbe Sound. It skipped once then sank.

Chapter Eighteen

"You know we're supposed to call it Settlement Island now," she said. "Flywell had too many bad connotations."

"So it's good for you now? Like a resort?"

She turned away. "That's the idea. To cure whatever ills you."

CHAPTER NINETEEN

That afternoon two men built like boxcars set up shop in front of the Swill's door. One man had blonde hair, the other brown. They'd brought along thermoses of coffee, liverwurst sandwiches, and two wood stakes fastened with signs, one saying "sinners," the other "heathens." Under each man's coat was a crucifix, a prayer book, and a .36 snub-nosed revolver. At the sounding of the smelting factory's 2pm bell, these men finished their sandwiches, took a slug of coffee, and then began pacing in synchrony before the Swill's door, chanting, "Booze destroys families. God hates drink."

Lily saw them first. She and Joshua were passing the florist when she stopped short and pointed. "Christ, Jesus is here."

Joshua moved ahead of her, wanting to get to the men a good ten feet before she arrived. He lowered his hat, kept his palms out of his pockets, and looked each of them over. When he was convinced he couldn't take either in a fight if they were both drunk and crippled, he gave them a genial smile.

"Buy you fellas a drink?"

The blonde turned and spit.

"Beat it," he said. "Got our boss the same as you got your boss so let's try not to get all close or nothing. You know how it goes."

His partner nodded in agreement.

"All I offered was a free drink," Joshua said. "Not trying to court you."

The brown-haired one pointed at the sign. "Can't you read, buddy. We stopped drinking to get good with God."

Lily stopped beside him. She looked at the signs and then the men and then back at the signs. "This is all so dramatic. Why don't you just ask for the money in a quiet fashion?"

"Sorry, lady," said the blonde one. "Don't mean to make it hard on a pregnant broad, even if she's Jew pregnant, but we got our orders like you got your orders so let's not make it personal or nothing."

"Jew pregnant?" she said.

"Don't take it that way," the dark one said. "He don't mean nothing by it."

"Tell Vanderhock I've got no money for him," Joshua said. "Barely scraping by as it is."

They shrugged. These guys, Joshua realized, weren't Joel's collection plate.

"What does he want then?" Joshua asked.

"For us to stand right here holding these here signs and make sure no one goes in without hearing from us first," the blonde one said.

Joel's thugs were doing a hell of a job at that. Downstairs there was only Rafael standing behind the bar drinking a glass of red wine, a pistol visible under his coat.

"It has been a very slow day, even by this year's standard."

Joshua opened the till and found a fifty-cent piece.

"Some man in the privy," Rafael said. "Would you like for me to show the men upstairs the way to the Sound, see if they float like witches of yore?"

"They called me Jew pregnant," Lily said. "Like I'm carrying the antichrist."

"Vermin," Rafael said. "If you'll excuse me, I will go hear their dying words."

Lily hugged Rafael. "We don't need to murder anyone today. Besides I'm sure their mothers love them."

"Men like that do not have mothers," Rafael said. "They fell to Earth ugly and dim."

Joshua went to the kitchen to make Lily lunch, while Rafael followed. In the icebox, Joshua found a piece of liver and then dropped it on the hot griddle, while Rafael whispered, "Why is Vanderhock suddenly interested in our tavern? It seems as though he has richer places to extort."

"My guess is Olive." He buttered some bread and laid it on a cooler part of the griddle. "Have you seen her?"

"No. What did she do?"

"She wasn't telling me the whole truth a few months back, about the job."

"Of course she was not. The girl has never met a truth that hasn't growled when she bends down for a pet."

Joshua told him about the meeting with Jasper Smythe, how the man-who-would-be-mayor had threatened Lily and the baby, because, Joshua figured, Olive had conned Jasper along the way. She'd probably done the same to Vanderhock.

"Those names," Rafael said. "Smythe, Vanderhock. Far too much history and blood."

"And just over a painting," Joshua said. "You remember it? You're in—"

"No."

Chapter Nineteen

Rafael said it in a way that made sure Joshua didn't think of pressing for more information.

"Be careful," Rafael said. "The Smythes have been a pile upon the ass of this Island since there was nothing but cows and smallpox."

"I know the stories."

"Not all of them, you do not," Rafael said. "Whenever I have believed that I have mastered this town, the ground has torn open beneath my feet."

Joshua was about to chide the old man for being silly—history didn't matter in a town that knocked down every shred of it to put up something taller and newer—but stopped when Lily shrieked from the bar. He picked up a chef's knife and Rafael followed with his gun into the front of the house to find Lily hugging a man in a trench coat, a camera case slung over his shoulder.

The man gave a friendly nod with a smirk that had probably got him punched a dozen times.

"Rivers," Lily said. "This is an old friend of mine, Neal Stephens. We knew each other back, back—"

"Back when we were younger," Neal said, while looking at Joshua's knife, Rafael's gun. "A long time ago, especially for me. Like I said, your wife and I are old friends."

"Like you told him? Wait. Rivers, you never mentioned Neal had come by."

"It was a misunderstanding," Neal said. "Me and your husband just had a quick talk. I guess I came across as a bit shifty."

Joshua didn't know what to make of this guy. You didn't come into a man's bar and hug his pregnant wife unless you were a prodigal brother or a long-lost cousin and this guy was neither. Joshua knew Lily had old boyfriends, but he didn't know they were rich and handsome.

"Nice to meet you, again Neal. Get you a drink?" Joshua said.

Chapter Nineteen

"Whiskey, your best."

Neal dropped a five on the bar, enough for two bottles of the Swill's best. Joshua buried the bill deep in the till and then grabbed the cheapest whiskey in the house. No label. Just a brown liquid distilled in a backyard.

"Enjoy."

"Rivers, you're a son of a bitch," Lily said.

Neal took a sniff of it, shut his eyes, and grimaced before the sip but took it all down just the same.

"Excellent." He held open his mouth for a beat to let the fumes escape. "Best I've ever had."

"I'm sorry, Neal," Lily said. "Rivers is just—"

She lost her sentence when the door opened and down the steps stomped cheap patent loafers and wide cuffed slacks. Joshua laid the knife in the sink and his palms on the bar. When the guy reached the landing, he surveyed the lot of them: a red-headed barman, his pregnant wife, a pretty photographer in need of a beating, and an old man in a fine suit holding a pistol with no intention of putting it away. If the scene rattled the man, he didn't show it. He appeared a hard 50 on days he shaved, but this wasn't one of those. There was a coffee stain on his shirt and his tie had come unknotted. On first glance, Joshua thought he looked just like any other Irish cop—and there were no other kinds in Port Kydd—but the way he held himself worried Joshua. This guy was a thinker.

Neal pointed at the stranger. "He's a cop, right?"

"Who's this idiot?" the cop said.

"Can I take your picture?" Neal said. He was already opening his camera case when Lily put a hand on him.

"Sit and be quiet," Lily said.

"Thanks, ma'am." The cop turned to Joshua. "Did you a favor and chased off the goons upstairs. Thought their shaming might be bad for business."

Chapter Nineteen

Joshua nodded.

"Getting a real sense of warmth about this place, yes, a generosity of spirit," the cop said, glancing over at the walls, but somehow keeping track of Rafael's gun.

"Figure I should display this." The cop pulled out a badge. "Identification of an officer of the court is one way to avoid anarchy. Detective Sergeant John Duffy."

He turned toward Rafael. "I've got a gun too."

"Your mother must be proud," Rafael said.

Duffy laughed. "You're everything I always heard you were, Mr. Castillo. Right down to those pretty eyes."

"You're too kind," Rafael said. "But do you have a warrant for this intrusion or are you simply here for some afternoon extortion?"

Joshua came around the bar and stepped in front of Rafael. There was no accounting for stray bullets and pregnant women.

"You're Joshua Rivers," Duffy said.

It wasn't a question.

"What's this about, officer?" Joshua said.

"Well, what the hell do you think?"

PART THREE: THE MARBLE GRAVEYARD

CHAPTER TWENTY

<u>December 6, 1873</u>

For Billy-Bailey Vanderhock, the great swell of bronze birds was nothing less than a vindication of his years in the wilderness. The scorn of sinners, his trial. The birds, his reward. He recalled how ravens brought Elijah food; how doves signaled to Noah the end of the flood; how Psalms mentioned something about swallows…he couldn't remember. But no matter. Here was his lightning strike on the road to Damascus. Those sinners thought him a false prophet, just as they did Ezekiel. Or Jeremiah. He easily confused them. But look at them now, all of them to parish in a blaze of righteous glory.

He had come to the Bonny that morning to call upon God to strike down the evil barmaid carrying a bastard. That an unwed woman could own a house serving the Devil's brew and carry the Devil's spawn in her womb struck at the very heart of the Bonny's sins. And to Billy-Bailey, the Bonny was the Earth's most evil house. And to speak on this holy day, a feast for a papist deity like St. Nicholas, further set his heart afire. For hours, he had stood on a milk crate, quoting Deuteronomy, "A bastard shall not enter into the congregation of the Lord."

Chapter Twenty

No one paid him much attention. Sidewalk preachers were as common in the Bonny as bed bugs. It was just something everyone had to tolerate.

So when the thunder arrived, a great rattle of the Earth like that of *Revelations*, Billy-Bailey turned to the west and cried for joy. The end times had finally arrived. The storm was a harbinger of sulfur that would rain down upon the unfaithful.

"Let the Heathens burn!" he cried.

A woman stopped beside him. She wore a long green dress and looked like the paintings of the Virgin Mary. He was transfixed. This was the first sign, he thought. An angel. But when she looked up with dark eyes, he fell off his milk crate and into the slop.

"You!"

"Me," the woman said.

She was old like Noah, like Enoch. The oldest woman he had ever seen. Do not be cowered by the devil in false dress, he thought. So he stood, pushing up against her, acting as one of Christ's chosen warriors.

"Not talking to you but yes now you know who I am because I've been coming for you for centuries yes I have because I am Charlemagne I am the Crusades I am the Knight of New Rotterdam!" he cried.

His lips foamed, blued. Gunshots nearby. He dared not turn away.

"You are a madman, little one," the woman said. Her words shot violence into his veins, hate into his heart. Good hate, he thought. The hate that saved his soul. He took a long breath and then gave the sermon he had long prepared for when faced with the devil.

"Am I? ha! this whole world is this way because of you and your kind you see? you who seek change who live outside the laws of Anglo decency you been coming at us for centuries ever since Saul's crown was taken and that's where it began you and the Seminoles and the Barbarians and the Romans and the Celts and the Quakers and the Gnostics and the Jews and the Princes of Mormonhood and Muhammad and Buddha and Vishnu and the Epicureans and the Spartans and the Mongols and the Mayans with your worshipping of Augustus and Thomas Wyatt and Galileo and de Sade and Christopher Marlowe and Alexander Hamilton and that harlot Dolley Madison and you tell us it's the Masons and it is but they're only part of you because the world is ending because masturbation causes madness and the world is flat and the sun circles us and the redheads will die out in the fire and the whole lot of you want to take our land yes that's what I said it's our land just like them greedy Smythes have done and you want to turn us into slaves and turn Billy-Bailey into a God-hating pagan but I ain't going to do it because my Daddy taught me this was my city and he taught me to fight to reclaim it and so here's Billy-Bailey a soldier from the depths of New Rotterdam and now you come here in the deep dark night and expect me to bow down and worship your devil on *my* island but I won't do it you see because I know how to exorcise you yes you the old woman of the Bonny."

Gunshots followed and then a cry sent his eyes east, where, before him stood a Black child looking down upon the torn head of a slain white man. He turned back but the woman in green had disappeared. Back to hell, he figured. And he also knew the fight had begun for the army of the devil shall rise to defend this Sodom and only God's angels would stand in protection.

Billy-Bailey had brought his sword, or, more accurately, a Colt .31. It was heavy in hand, much too large for a man so small, and he often missed his target, but on this day of judgment he knew himself to be as strong as Michael during the fall.

"Kill the heathens!" he said.

And so he fired.

CHAPTER TWENTY-ONE

<u>October 23, 1929—Port Kydd, USA</u>

Duffy asked him to come for a walk so Joshua took a walk. Up top and under the bright, cold sun Joshua followed Duffy, while trying to stay a step behind him so it didn't look like they were talking, because the street was watching, making sure Joshua hadn't turned snitch.

A streetcar rattled past and Duffy pointed at an old livery stable turned car barn. He said, "That's where the Blackbeards used to congregate. Fiercest gang in town before they got got. Your friend Castillo was rumored to have done the deed."

"That's a nice story," Joshua said. "Glad you told me."

"Well, there's no call to be an asshole about it."

When they reached the border of Little Holland, they stopped beside a fire station, across the street from Vanderhock's church. It was made of white timber and stuccoed brickwork, with three chimneys, the kind of building you found in the oldest parts of downtown.

"Back in the day, that was a printer's shop. And when I say back in the day, I mean way back when there was no American flag flying. It was owned by a fellow named Johann Vanderhock.

He ran a press that was for the British one day and then the Americans the next. A real patriot. God those people been sons of bitches since Adam first felt up Eve."

Joshua shrugged.

"Real talker, you are. Just blab until you're blue in the face."

"I don't get what—"

"Old Johann never saw the end of the war. Got himself got as well, if you know what I mean. Poison. Real dark arts sort of witchcraft. Rumor has it that it was his little Irish servant girl named Rivers who'd done it. Story sound familiar?"

It did. It was one of the stories told to men who thought about messing with Rivers women. They were lethal, everyone said. Black widows. It was why all their children were bastards.

"Well," Joshua said, "sometimes little servant girls have ideas of their own."

"Hell, little servant girls can change history. Just interesting that you and the Vanderhocks go back that far."

"It was a small town back then."

A wave of cars sped past and then with a break in the traffic Duffy crossed over to the Marble Graveyard. The gate was busted, so Duffy stepped over, dusted off his trousers and turned to Joshua, who was glued to the sidewalk, even as the tide of the crowd tried to push him down the road.

Behind Duffy stood rows of marble sarcophaguses, all above ground to protect against the floods that occasionally swept over from the Crabbe Sound and drowned the city in a foot of water. Some said the graveyard was haunted. Others believed it was home to a haven of rattlesnakes, even though there were no snakes on Port Kydd, all of them driven out, the history books said, by Jefferson Smythe in 1720. Someone had ignored these rumors and gone ahead and painted a cock and balls along the side of the nearest sarcophagus.

Chapter Twenty-One

"I get paid by the day," Duffy said. "So let's move it along, will you? No ghosts in here. Not really."

Joshua followed Duffy through the filled-up graveyard. There was hardly an empty tract left for the future, though he *knew* there was room for a couple more dead. It was amazing, Joshua thought, in this time and place that these two acres hadn't somehow been dug up by the bankers.

Duffy was thinking the same thing.

"About ten years back the city got a bright idea from some banker to use eminent domain and take the land and put up some more shit tenements. Then it all falls apart because the banker and the city clerk and the mayor went out on the Crabbe for some pleasure boat whoring and the damn boat sunk. None of the bodies were ever found, swallowed, you see, by the wrath of the Crabbe. All very biblical. You remember this?"

"No."

"Not much for superstition myself, but I've seen some strange things. Reminds me of this story my Ma used to tell me when I was kid. That each neighborhood on the Island has her own god looking out for it, but like the Greek Gods, they're finicky, somewhat human, prone to lust and vengeance. Give a shit about some things but not others. She said the Graaf Street god wore a tie and the Little Holland god wore wooden shoes but that the Bonny god was a woman. Odd the myths that stick with us."

Duffy stopped before a crypt that was about ten feet high and ten feet wide and ten feet long and had a sealed brass door that had an old-fashioned lever type lock, the kind you'd find at the front of a haunted house. Duffy pointed at the row of names carved into the plaque beside the door.

Siobhan Rivers ?—1826
Margaret Rivers 1784—1840
Louisa Rivers 1824—1871

Chapter Twenty-One

Eleanor Rivers 1850—1924
Margaret Rivers 1874—1905
Joshua Rivers 1894—
Olive Rivers 1899—

Joshua hadn't laid flowers for his grandmother, hadn't stepped foot here since he was 11 years old.

"Something, ain't it?" Duffy said. "Seeing your name up there. It's got to be hard for you, knowing where you're going to end up. Though a wise man once said, 'Dying is a wild night and a new road.'"

"You come prepared with that quote?" Joshua said.

Duffy pointed toward the south wall. "So you know about these as well, right?"

On a smaller crypt, with a smaller door, there was a smaller plaque.

Jude Kelly 1845—1873
Rafael Estèban Miguel Castillo 1847—
Lucille Rose Castillo 1845—1918

Duffy began walking. The weeds deepened further into the graveyard, reaching all the way up to his coat pockets.

"What's this about?" Joshua asked. "You want me to say I don't want to be here? You're right, I don't. You want to hang around with your dead?"

Duffy pointed toward a crypt two rows down. "That's where my parents lay. Grew up here, same as you."

"Sorry," Joshua said. "Just don't see the point of places like this. Should just burn us when we're done and throw the ashes in the garbage."

"Yeah, a lot of us who came back from Europe say the same thing. Look, I just want the truth. Some cops are fine with just a motive and a weapon. Sometimes they don't even need that, but I've got to have the story. The 'whys' that ain't apparent with just a witness and a warm gun."

Chapter Twenty-One

Duffy pulled out a notebook and then began reciting the Rivers' family Christmas card.

"Let's see here. Far as I can tell your family shows up in this country in 1775. That little Irish servant girl we were talking about, Sy-o-bahn, See-o-ban Rivers—."

"Shi-vawn. The 'bh' sounds like a 'v.'"

"That don't make sense in any language. Anyways, I had some guys at the library dig up some old newspaper clippings, some history books and the like and found out she was a prisoner during the war. Spy and murderess, it says here."

Joshua lit a cigarette, gave a no-fucks shrug. "Pretty sure the statute of limitations is up on that."

"Just hold on, will you? You ain't got anywhere to be that'll do you any good. See there's a pattern here."

Joshua paused before a glimmer in the grass. He crouched, his hands wrapping around something cold and metallic, and came up with a rusted pistol. He showed it to Duffy.

"Uh, just wipe your fingerprints off of it and toss it back."

Joshua did. They walked on.

"Well, after her, seems like your family settled in, watched the neighborhood grow up around them. A whole lot of mothers and daughters, but not many fathers, far as I can see."

"Being a bastard isn't a crime, anymore."

"No, but it fits a pattern. Well, seems like you all stayed out of any real trouble, nothing but a bunch of petty larcenies and license forgeries but then your grandmother came along, the one whose paintings have got everyone worked up."

"Everyone?" Joshua said. "I thought it was just you getting curious after the painting showed up?"

"Nah, ain't me who put you in the muck now. Smythe called the Chief who called my Captain who called me. A landslide of worked-up shit heading downhill, and you're at the bottom, if I don't say. Can I keep going?"

Chapter Twenty-One

Joshua lit a cigarette.

"Well your grandmother was a no one until recently. Apparently, she's all of a sudden a favorite of bohemians and bored suffragists. Paintings quadrupling in price. A hard-to-find artist since all her surviving work was bought up by Smythe's mother." Duffy peered over his notebook. "Did you know that?"

"Not until today."

"Another friend of your family, that guy Kelly, couldn't pass a bank without robbing it. Now your Ma had a rap sheet ranging from counterfeiting to owning a vicious dog. Can't find anything on your father, though. Again, fits the pattern."

Duffy stopped by the Avery sarcophagus and then flipped the page of his notebook.

"Let's see, what else, what else. Oh, here's my favorite, your friend Mr. Castillo has wreaked some serious havoc. The Comstock agents tried to get him for years but he never got got. Some robberies dating back fifty years, a few dead bodies. How he's still alive is beyond me. Now this brings us to your sister, who seems to be keeping this grand tradition alive. She's been picked up at least twenty times for playing every sort of game I can think of. Always beat the charges, though. And finally there's you."

"No convictions."

"But there's a couple of guys bruised up in Montana say there should be. Christ, your family crest must be a pair of handcuffs."

Duffy looked waxed.

"Don't matter much anyhow. Your wife seems to have cleaned you up, except for running a speak, but that ain't a real crime."

Joshua stopped at the entrance. They had circled around and had nowhere else to go. He leaned against the wall and felt as tired as he had in years.

"Detective, get to it."

Chapter Twenty-One

"Well," Duffy began, "you could say it's the distribution of power in America and the use of her police force to maintain that power, but you don't care about that do you? Not a philosopher, I can tell. So I'll tell you what I need and frankly what you need and that's your sister and we sure as shit can't find her."

"No word at all?"

"Yeah, we got word. All kinds. Some guy saw her in Cooke Village, another spotted her near the Armory, a third in Herhalling of all godforsaken places, but that ain't the same as having her."

"I haven't seen her in a year."

"You should probably learn to lie a little better than that. Look, I've been tasked by the citizenry to uphold her laws, no matter how silly those laws may be so I do this for eleven dollars a day and I need that eleven dollars to feed my mean wife and fat children and the Chief is threatening to take that away from me unless I make an arrest in the matter of this painting so I get yanked off two murders to chase after oil on canvas. Christ, this city wouldn't know justice if it came over and fondled her tits."

"If the other paintings turn up, can we all forget this ever happened?"

"Normally sure. Save the taxpayers the trouble, but not on this one because there hasn't been one goddamn honest thing in this case."

Duffy explained that the detective who'd handled the initial robbery had only bothered to interview the witnesses—Raab, the two night watchmen, and the beaten-up cop—and hadn't even photographed the scene. No fingerprints taken, no follow-up the next day. No one cared. Not even Jasper.

"So why all the interest now? One painting's been found. That's a good thing, isn't it?"

Chapter Twenty-One

Duffy looked away. He knew the same thing Joshua did. That *The Passenger Pigeons* wasn't ever supposed to show up again. That was the problem. The robbery was secondary. Now someone had to take the fall, preferably someone small and poor.

"Look," Duffy said. "I don't give a Bonny fuck if your sister knocked over the library and, frankly, if you helped her, but if I can't find another asshole to take the fall or Smythe doesn't lose interest soon, I'll have to keep looking at her and if she ain't around I've been told to cuff the next best thing and guess who that is?"

"Justice, right?"

"You said it, brother."

CHAPTER TWENTY-TWO

By the time Duffy let him go, it was sunset so Joshua bought a bottle from a beat cop and started walking through the mob of sagging fedoras and torn nylons. Back at the Swill there'd be the suspicious eyes of his wife who was probably being consoled by her ex-lover and he didn't want to look at either of them. At a line of pay phones, he checked his pockets but he'd spent his last nickel on the bottle so he kept walking. It didn't matter. What was there left to say to Lily? It had to be as obvious to her as it was to him that they were plainly fucked.

He stepped into a doorway and let the liquor wash down his throat. The first sip burned but the second felt just right. He moved on, walking until he crossed into the Jewish Quarter where his welcoming party greeted him. A familiar blonde came up behind him, pressed her pistol against his back and told him to walk regular.

"Like we're going on a little date."

"Haven't we met before?"

"You got a good memory. Saw you ways back at Mags' Hangout."

"That's right. You offered to give me a suck. Now you're pulling a gun. Graduated I see."

"Mister, you got a mouth on you."

"You're not going to kill me here," Joshua said.

"Why not?" she said, looking around. "See any cops?"

She led him into an alleyway that smelled like burnt trash and then pointed at an old idling Ford, the kind you had to crank. When he got in, the driver turned around and he saw it was Molly.

"I thought we were friends?" he said, relaxing.

Molly drove off, looping around the city, wandering in no particular direction, up to Knight City Park and then down along the Crabbe all the way through Chinatown and Graaf Street before turning north and parking under the elevated train on the border separating Little Holland and Pinebox Square. Molly pointed across the road at an old Victorian gone flophouse. They led him across the street, guns out in the open, neither bothering to look for cops. The folks nearby, people sleeping on the sidewalk or passing a pipe in a doorway, looked anywhere else but at him. No one wanted to swear in court to seeing him die, though, by then, he wasn't the least bit worried about the pair of them unless they were more doped up than they let on. They pushed through the door and into a dark entranceway that was hot and damp from the churning boiler. The ceiling was built in a sort of horseshoe arch, decorated in blue ceramic tiles. He wanted to loosen his tie but the blonde was fidgety, nervous.

The heat eased when they came upstairs into a converted railroad apartment with a hot plate, an icebox, and a mattress on the floor. He found a pair of chairs facing one another and Molly pointed her pistol at one and told him to sit. He sat.

He offered them the bottle but they had already gone.

Chapter Twenty-Two

The room seemed to go on for a good forty feet. There was a north-facing window that led to a thirty-foot drop and no fire escape. In the fireplace, a few old coals remained along with some spent cigarette butts and the corpse of the largest rat he'd ever seen, something fit for a zoo. There was a chemical stink, kind of like paint thinner. Near the toilet sat a vase full of dead flowers, roses it looked like. As footsteps made their way up the stairs, he unscrewed his bottle and then turned to offer his sister a drink.

"No thanks, big brother," Olive said. "A girl's got to keep her head in a neighborhood teeming with all sorts of criminal types."

She gave him a cold kiss on the cheek and then went to the other chair, dusted it off, and then sat, crossing her legs, an elbow on her knee, hand holding up her chin. She wore a dirty white dress like a bride thrown from her honeymoon car.

"Why send your girls after me?" he asked. "Could have just called."

"Joanie's just the help. Give a girl a dollar and a gun, she'll do what you ask. Give the same to a man, he's liable to get ideas. I don't like the help having ideas. But you should be nicer to Molly. She said you hurt her feelings sneering at her like that."

"Your *friend's* gun hurt mine."

"Friend? Joshua, really?"

He leaned in, whispered, "This isn't like you. Don't you trust me?"

"Don't you think you're being tailed?"

He hadn't seen anyone but hadn't been looking either.

"Joshua, Joshua, Joshua—what are you doing? You're off talking to cops and lunching with Jasper Smythe."

"What?"

"Jasper Smythe. Rich fellow, sloppy suit."

"Christ, how long have your girls been following me?"

"Why Jasper?"

"He called *me* and had me come up to the library, just so he could threaten me. Do you think I've turned snitch? I'm your goddamn brother."

She didn't tell him to cut it out, to stop yelling, to get ahold of himself. She simply said, "Go on." He'd put up with enough today, been threatened three times and kept his mouth shut but as he looked at the flophouse with the giant rat and the vase of roses and the girls just out of sight, he knew, in fact, that he was also just the help.

So he spilled, going over every detail of meeting Jasper, of the librarian Raab, and of the mercenary Hess. He told her about Vanderhock's men outside of his door and about Detective Duffy and that this investigation was coming down from up high and after a while when it seemed she'd stopped listening, he banged his foot on the floor and she looked up, bored.

"We're in over our heads," he said.

"Which painting?" she asked.

"*The Passenger Pigeons.*"

"No, where did they find it?"

"With some guy named Harlan Law, why?"

"That's good."

"Jesus, Olive, aren't you listening? We've got to run."

She went to the icebox and took out a bottle of tomato juice and then drank straight from the jug.

"Jasper," Joshua said. "He hired you to steal them, right, for the insurance?"

She took another drink and then returned it to the icebox before wiping her lips with a handkerchief.

"You double-crossed him?" Joshua asked. He paused as a siren came down the street only to pass out of earshot. "And same goes for Vanderhock, right? And probably this Harlan Law?"

"Just forget about it. It's in the bag, big brother. In the bag. Couple of days it will all blow over but until then just keep your head low."

Joshua went to the fireplace. The charred rat looked like a possum who had taken to the bottle. Even in the trenches, they'd never gotten that big. He was about to ask of it, but figured she'd just lie. So he started for the stairs: "You know I love you. There isn't anything I wouldn't do for you. If you killed a guy, I'd sink the body."

"I know," she said. "I'm sorry for all of this."

She didn't mean it. Whatever was going on, he thought it had warped Olive in some indefinable way.

"Take care of yourself," he said. "But I've got to watch out for my wife and kid and that might mean leaving town for a while."

"I'm sure you will. You're good at that."

CHAPTER TWENTY-THREE

When he got back to the Swill it was long after dark, hours after he'd left with Duffy, and he was in for it from Lily. He came downstairs to find a small cloud of old men drinking, while Lily poured beers for those two goons from earlier and the Reverend Joel Vanderhock.

"Good evening, Rivers," Joel said, raising his mug. "I hope you're having a fine day."

"Yeah, it's been fantastic. Didn't think you were a drinking man."

"This is their third round," Lily said. "Apparently if they bless the beer, it's sacramental."

She threw her towel and went into the kitchen and Joshua followed, reaching out but before he could touch her, she turned and punched him in the chest.

"You want to tell me where you've been?"

"Look, Duffy—"

"Save it for whoever you have on the side."

"Stop it. Where's Neal?"

She turned up the stairs.

"I'm sorry," Joshua called before the door slammed. He lit a cigarette, took a long drag over the simmering soup, and then returned to the bar, where he told Vanderhock to go jerk himself.

"That's not very hospitable, Rivers," Joel said.

"What did you tell her?" Joshua said.

"I just congratulated her on the coming child and said it was a shame that the babe would be raised in a den of iniquity, that the Lord forgives sinners once they repent, but punish the wicked, like your deviant of a sister, but sometimes there are accidental casualties in the battle for the Lord."

Joel took a drink of his ale like a man with a lot of practice. He pulled up a beer towel and ran it along his lip. Behind him, the old men got up, fixed their hats, and left a dime on the table. Not one looked at Joshua as they headed up the stairs.

"Olive's got a choice," Joel said before draining his beer. When he came up for air, his eyes flared like the hangman's before the drop. "She either comes clean with what she owes me or she gives me back my money."

"There a third choice?"

"I think we both know the third choice." Joel picked up his hat. "Rivers, you know your sister's rotten, but your wife isn't. Think about what helping Olive gets you. Think about what it costs the rest of your family. I'd hate to see your home turned timber over old grudges."

CHAPTER TWENTY-FOUR

After closing, Joshua lingered at the window beside the bedroom door. On his first cigarette, the lamps of a police car cut through the darkness, illuminating a stevedore sleeping under a pile of torn sails. On his second cigarette, a couple fell out of Pirate's Alley, her on top, and she kept bouncing, even as men from a nearby tavern stepped out to watch. On his third cigarette, Miss Amand rounded the corner on a donkey, a cowboy hat over her bonnet, a cigar in her mouth, looking like Pancho Villa's long-lost grandmother. It was that type of night, he thought, the kind where old dreams came to you in the form of prophecies. For six months he'd pushed down the memory of the robbery, tried to forget about it, but for six months he suspected that it was just a matter of time before it burst up like a geyser. He felt the worry in his peeling hands and cranky back, in the memories he kept losing and the ones he couldn't lose. And he felt it on the cold side of his mattress when he went to bed.

He could tell by the irregular beat of her breath, the way her hair fell onto the pillow gracefully, rather than in a mess, that she was awake, waiting.

"We got to make some choices," he said, hesitating. "These aren't the kind of men you grew up with. When they say they'll do something, they mean it."

Orla came up on the bed, curled into Lily's thigh, and fell asleep.

"They don't care that you're pregnant or that you've got nothing to do with this."

Then, when she didn't say anything, when he wasn't sure she was *hearing* him, he did something neither expected. He told her the truth.

He told her that he'd helped Olive rob the library, that he hadn't known at first that it was his grandmother's paintings, but that he made three grand off the job. He told her that Jasper Smythe had hired Olive to do it so he could collect the insurance money and that she'd snitched on the guy who'd actually bought the painting. He told her that he had no idea why she did that, except that it probably put Jasper in a bind with his insurance company and maybe it threw his mayoral campaign into disarray. He told her that Olive had probably promised Vanderhock the painting or sold him a forgery. He wasn't sure. And he told her that Duffy was looking to pin the job on Olive, and if he couldn't get her, Joshua was next in line.

"You want me to keep talking?"

"I stopped listening a while ago."

She pulled the lamp chain. Light cast over the left side of her face, illuminating puffy, wet eyes. The right of her face remained dark.

"I knew you robbed the library, like I've known about all of your other petty crimes since day one. You think I'm stupid? I just didn't *want* to know, to really know."

"I'm sorry."

"Don't talk. Not wanting to know is my fault, but you're up to your eyeballs in it. You've got to get out of this mess. You hear me? You've got to be a man and clean up your mess. You think you're tough? Prove it. Save your skin. I don't care how you do it and if you feel like you got to tell me how, then you do it if that's what you need because I don't care how you do it. Hear me? If that means flipping on your nutjob of a sister, you do it."

"Lily, we've got to run. We've got to."

"Stop it. Stop it. Stop it." She slapped the pillows. "I'm not leaving. You hear me? I'm not. This is my home."

"These guys—"

"Look, Jasper Smythe is a millionaire, not a killer. Vanderhock is a preacher. Sure, he's bent but that doesn't make him a killer either. All you've got to worry about is the cops and there's a way to fix it. That detective said all he wants is your sister, right?"

"You don't know these guys, their history."

"Stop being so scared. Hell, I thought you were made of more than that. I didn't bring this mess home. You did. You and your crazy sister. You're going to cut her off, Rivers. You have to. I don't want her around our baby. I can't have our baby turning into someone like her."

"Lily—"

"She's sick and runs around with sick little girls and I don't want my baby turning into someone like her, or, hell, like your mom or your grandmother either and all their bitterness and anger because I don't want her running away from us like you did. You all put so much goddamn weight on each other and I don't want that for her. The dead don't get a say on how my baby lives."

"I can't just let Olive get hurt."

"Olive's a big girl," she said. "You think you're tough? Do something tough then. I didn't think I married a guy who jumped at his own shadow."

Chapter Twenty-Four

She went to the sink and splashed water on her face. Her paisley nightgown fit like a sack over her alarming size. Any day now, the doctor had told her.

"Lily."

She held her hand up. She was done listening. In the mirror he caught her eye and sat up. There was a curdle to her face, a sort of sneer he'd never seen before, like how you'd look at a soldier caught deserting. A mix of disgust and pity. He'd wanted to tell her about California, about the island where you could watch the whales, about how they could make a quiet, peaceful life out there, but he was afraid of what she'd say. He was afraid to ever see that look on her face again.

CHAPTER TWENTY-FIVE

The mid-morning sunlight sank into the glazed terracotta towers, as if it was fueling the building's electric lights, feeding her worker bees, those artists of law briefs and stock reports, the heart-blood of the capitalist system. Financial photosynthesis. At the foot of those twenty-story towers, you found remnants of Old Port Kydd, the Island of the American Revolution. Three-story federalist buildings of yellow brick that used to house courts and legislatures. Gothic churches crafted from limestone, guarded by gargoyles. Graveyards populated with Dutch names. All the while men in double-breasted suits and women in three-inch heels went about their business, marching in formation down the sidewalk, oblivious to the beauty and history surrounding them, passing through time unaware of the creeping end.

Or at least that's how Neal Stephens described Graaf Street. Camera to his eye, he expounded upon the majesty of the old neighborhood nestled up next to the new. Lily—her own camera at the ready—agreed.

"I love it down here," she said. "It's as though you've stepped back in time."

"It's more than that though, isn't it?" Neal said. "It's like time has caught up with you or as if history never really disappeared. Ooh, look."

Next to a newspaper stand lay a man dressed as Santa Claus, passed out. There was a bottle of "hair tonic" on his lap and a stench of gin wafting from his long, white beard. Lily and Neal both raised their cameras.

"A little early for Christmas," Neal said.

"Maybe he lost a bet."

"Or his marbles," Neal said. "I used to drink with a guy who dressed up as Abe Lincoln, you know with the top hat and chin strap, and was so utterly convinced he was the President that he refused to go to theaters."

They were wrong, Joshua knew. It wasn't like that at all. In 1826, a group of the "better" Irish, the kind who'd saved their money and started businesses, formed the Saint Nicholas Club. This secret society built a lodge just off Graaf Street with a hewn stone front and a door carved with the all-knowing eye, so that it looked vaguely Masonic. The club operated like most of its ilk, offering help to members in trouble, charity to the needy, and a fully stocked bar. Somehow the society's Christian origins warped, and now, during their monthly meetings, members dressed up as St. Nick, red robe and all, while drinking whatever they could get their hands on. This Santa Claus was a member who just needed a nap on his way home.

"Yeah it's odd," Joshua agreed. "Really odd."

Neal smiled as if surprised Joshua could speak. Lily looked at her nails. She hadn't wanted Joshua to come along but he'd insisted, saying it wasn't safe for her to be out in the city alone, not with everyone after him.

"Neal will be with me."

"Neal have a gun? Let's take him down to Graaf Street. He'll like that. Besides, I've never come along with you on one these camera trips of yours."

"It's work. You make it sound like bird watching."

There was nothing to say to make her feel better, so Joshua just hung back, following the pair through the old streets, hands in his pockets, mouth mostly shut as they took pictures of strangers who'd agreed to pose in "metaphorical" locations. Neal called himself a "photographer of faces," whatever the hell that meant.

"There's a specific look to the people here," he said as they walked over the footbridge that crossed Van Dyke stream. Joshua looked down at the water and saw a dead cat.

"I know what you mean," Lily said. "Everyone is slightly slouched, always with their hands in their pockets, their eyes looking at the ground."

"Pickpockets," Joshua said. "We're scared of pickpockets."

Lily sighed.

"Interesting," Neal said. "Really says something about how a place can affect the very nature of the people. You hear men like Galton say it's all in the blood, but I don't see it. The soil of a city, or at least its type of concrete, seems to have as great an effect as our blood."

What a blowhard, Joshua thought. Neal was the type of guy like Roche who ran his mouth as if he'd written the dictionary. But he wasn't exactly like Roche. He wasn't a crook looking at each passing man to see if he could take him in a fight. In fact, there wasn't a hint of violence about Neal. He came from Colorado coal money, Lily said, but had been a newspaper photographer during the War. He hadn't fired a gun as far as Joshua knew. He was no tough guy. That she'd gone out with him back in the day didn't make a whole lot of sense to Joshua, not after how she'd acted last night.

Chapter Twenty-Five

He was thinking on this when he caught a glimpse of a silver Packard pulling to a stop in front of the Queen Anne Teahouse. The driver stepped out wearing a black suit and a boxer's shoulders. It was the right type of car, Joshua saw, and the right kind of muscle. The driver came around to the back and opened the door to let out a sharply dressed, blonde man followed by his rich employer. The blonde looked down the sidewalks and across the street, skimming the faces, searching for coat bulges, before leading his employer through the glass doors of the teahouse.

Joshua turned to find Neal and Lily making their way down the footbridge toward the park, talking low enough so he couldn't hear them over the sound of the stream. They walked closely, like they should be holding hands. As they passed under a pair of maples, Joshua reached them.

"I'm going to head back to the Swill," he said. "Get ready for the lunch shift."

"Thanks for suggesting this neighborhood," Neal said. "I'm sorry you couldn't stay longer. I'd like to talk to you about the bar a bit more. I really have a fondness for old bars and with Volstead, most have gone the way of the dodo."

He seemed to mean it, even shaking Joshua's hand.

"I'll see you at home," he said to Lily, who was already walking away.

Joshua went back over the footbridge and then down Graaf Street, feeling his breath slowing even as his pace quickened. He had checked the gun twice before leaving the Swill and couldn't risk taking it out to look a third time, not within this posh crowd. His boots tread soft against the sidewalk, his joints loose and hands dry. The walkers around him seemed to slow down as if the projector was running on a lower speed. Across the street at the Port Kydd Central Bank, some sort of commotion had raised eyes toward the sky. Stock slips fell from windows, fluttering like confetti, but it wasn't part of his mission so he kept his gaze straight ahead. Just before reaching the teahouse, he checked his reflection in a plate glass window. He smoothed out his coat, brushed off his collar and sleeves. The gun was hidden in his right coat pocket. He turned to the teahouse door, reaching out for the brass handle but stopped when the door opened and spit out the sharp-dressed blonde.

"Mr. Rivers, this is far enough," Hess said. "The confines of this establishment are, of such a state, that I feel you will be made uncomfortable."

Even separated by the door, you could hear the clatter of cups against saucers, all made of the kind of china you had to start a colonial war to afford. Under that sound was a second, deeper tone, a voice speaking with authority. It was a vain voice, Joshua thought.

"Were you planning on coming to him as he gave his speech and shooting him—bang, bang—like in the pictures?" Hess said. "You'll get blood on all those nice dresses."

Nice dresses. Old women talking opera as they sipped Earl Grey and ate crumpets. They worried over the state of their summer homes and the moral degradation of the poor.

"That would be shame," Hess said. "The electric chair seems quite cruel. In Austro-Hungary we use pole. It's like hanging but very convoluted. I prefer French guillotine, quick, makes point."

"More of a firing squad man myself."

"Do you not think through this assassination?"

"No assassination. I just wanted to ask a question."

"With a gun?"

"Helps with the answer."

Joshua reached into his coat, slowly, before coming up with a pack of cigarettes and offering one to Hess.

"No. Yellows skin."

"Can I ask you something?"

"As long as there is no gun needed for answer."

"Fair enough. I was wondering, do you like him? Jasper."

Hess took a moment, his eyes again searching the street, the old soldier never disappearing. A crowd had formed beneath the bank. They were looking up, but Joshua wouldn't risk looking away from Hess, even with so many witnesses.

"No, no I do not," Hess said. "He is vile man, Mr. Smythe. He is spoiled. Self-loving. Thin-skinned. Cruel to the weak. Believes himself a great man but knows in some part of his small mind that if born to different parents he'd have been abandoned like a runt. It is curse of nobility. The first king is majestic yet he sires simpletons. America has not had this problem until recently with your self-made men but now you are squandering it. Very much like Austria."

"Yet you fight for both?"

"I am soldier. I do as I am told by man who pays me. Be it a king or his spoiled son, I kill for him same."

Joshua heard in Hess' voice what he saw in his posture and felt the familiar pain in his leg.

"I killed for country," Joshua said, lowering his voice. "That's what they told me. Ten times, or at least those are the ones I remember."

"A good number," Hess said. "Not great, but not shameful."

"I was only there for eight months. You had four years."

"Three," Hess said. "The last year I was guest of your army. Decent food. Much better than the English would have served us with their taste for goat. I always had a fondness for Americans after that."

"Sometimes I miss Europe."

"I do not think you do. You have been—how do they say it?—out of game for a long while. You have much to lose."

Joshua was about to say something, when, from the teahouse, he caught the words, "the Smythes founded this city and we

139

shall make it, once again, our light on the hill," followed by polite, lace-gloved applause.

"A boaster," Hess said. "As you people say."

"Jackass works too."

"Yes, I remember that phrase. Popular with your soldiers."

A scream sent both men's eyes back to the bank, where they caught a glimpse of the last moment of a falling man's life, arms splayed out, before meeting the pavement, shaking the ground beneath their boots. Joshua felt his own eyes narrow, his own heart pick up.

Keep calm.

Keep calm.

Hess, on the other hand, seemed unaffected, as if it was just a squirrel run over by a car.

"Bad way to die," Joshua said. He took a long drag from his cigarette.

"There are worse."

"Maybe he caught his wife with another man."

"Foolish. Kill the man not yourself. Maybe kill wife as well," Hess said. "I hope it is over money. More dignified."

"You're probably right."

"But you have fondness for women, so I understand why you think that," Hess said.

Joshua had known Austrians during the War, men imprisoned, some in cages, and thought most of them weren't much different than the Americans, just guys caught up in the wrong moment in history, but others seemed bat-bitten, rabid. Depravation did that.

"What did you wish to ask my employer?" Hess said. "Perhaps I can answer it."

"What would it take to make peace?"

"Mr. Rivers, the only way this ends well for you is a bullet in the brain of your sister."

CHAPTER TWENTY-SIX

Rafael had gone ahead and opened the tavern for a trio of Poles in need of an early drink. They'd been laid off the week before from the Smythe ironworks and now sat at the long table reading over the want ads, their Trilbies low over their eyes, while nursing their beers like they were down to selling teeth. Rafael brought them bowls of potato soup and slices of bread.

"In gratis," he said. "May you find luck in your future."

Rafael turned to find Joshua pouring an ale.

"A little early, is it not?" Rafael said. "Is your lovely bride still entertaining her old friend?"

"They're taking pictures of bums and calling it art."

Rafael laughed over the sink while picking at a block of ice, an apron tied around his waist, his soft French cuffs rolled to the elbow. "My late Lucille had her own oddities. When we made love she only spoke in that ugly language of Gaelic, so that now, when I hear it, I find I must sit and wait for the spirit to pass."

Rafael went about his work, a trade he hated, but one he'd grown used to over the last five decades. Although he'd never had a regular shift at the Swill, he knew how to run the bar when it was called for. He just didn't particularly enjoy it unless he saw himself as a grand host to a bevy of illustrious guests. It took some imagination for him.

"You remember my grandmother when she painted?" Joshua asked. "We never talked about this."

Rafael poured another cup of coffee. "Some. I found her work, um, banal? When your mother was born, she had little time for it. Something must fall to the wayside."

He dipped a slice of bread in his coffee.

"But she liked it though?" Joshua said. "She was good at it people say."

"You saw her painting. What are your thoughts?"

"I don't know. I'm not the right person to say," Joshua said. "I'm just trying to figure out Olive's angle."

"You are better off consulting a fortune teller. I have no understanding of that child."

The phone rang. It was Ginny Styer, the baker from across the street.

"Honey, get out of there, now," she said. "The cops are outside."

Joshua hung up and looked out at Rafael and the Poles, at his poor, empty tavern and wondered, why here? But it wasn't a real question.

"Everyone out through the kitchen now."

Rafael reached for his gun.

"You too," Joshua said. "Find Lily."

"Come with us. There is no need for heroics."

"Nah, there isn't a fucking point. Go find, Lily, please."

Rafael herded the Poles past the oven and into the second pantry door, the one that led to the cavern. Joshua crouched behind the bar and swung open the trapdoor, tucking his gun right next to the money. He then smoothed out the bar mat.

What he'd told Rafael was true. There was no point in hiding. It would just make them angry.

It wasn't a minute before Detective Duffy slouched down the stairs, hat low, hands in his coat pockets, a real Bonny walk, followed by six uniformed officers. They hadn't bothered to pull their guns.

Duffy came up beside Joshua and sat on the neighboring stool.

"Awful sorry about this, Rivers."

"Jasper?"

"Looks like he's going to be the new mayor or at least that's what the fucking papers tell us but what man can really see the future? In any case the Chief thinks of himself as an oracle so he wants to be on the soft side of his future master. Says he's sorry too, though."

Duffy lit a cigarette and then handed it to Joshua.

"I really like this place," Duffy said. "It's got a good feel, like a man could retire in here. Sit all day, read the paper, and not talk if he didn't want to."

"It does have an old man feel to it."

"Yeah, it does," Duffy said. "Wife's not here, right? She is, we'll look the other way."

"Out at her bridge club."

Duffy pointed behind Joshua.

"We'll let the top shelves be, just bust up some of the shit bottles, turn over a few chairs. Should be fine once this blows over but we got to make it look like we tried in case Smythe's albino checks our work."

"Is this going to blow over?"

"Depends on your sister."

One of the cops came over with a blackjack. It looked warmed-over. Joshua didn't like where this was headed.

Chapter Twenty-Six

"I'll do it so it won't scar," Duffy said. "You're welcome to take a swing first if it makes you feel better. I won't hold it against you."

Joshua mashed out his cigarette and then thought of his daughter being born any day now.

"No, that's all right," Joshua said. "I know you don't mean it."

But Duffy swung hard enough that Joshua started thinking otherwise.

PART FOUR: THE TRAIN TO CALIFORNIA

CHAPTER TWENTY-SEVEN

December 6th, 1873

To Mary Smythe, the Bonny represented something nefarious, a place where women landed after making poor choices. It was a haven for gamblers, pirates, and the takers of young virtue. And therefore she found it a seductive evil. From birth, her life had been sequestered to tony Collier Park, amongst men who'd fought as officers during the Civil War, and women who spent their days drinking tea and praying. It was a righteous life, one of duty, far from the dregs of this lowly, filth-ridden site. But because of her isolation, she found the lurid particularly titillating. This fascination with the profane was a secret she scarcely admitted to herself. She first realized this predilection the previous summer in Paris, when her husband had taken her to the city morgue, one of the great tourist destinations. Thousands had lined up to get a look at the spectacle of the soulless. Her husband, Maynard, thought it was a crude exhibition, one only decadent Europeans could find appealing. But Mary loved it. It was so tactile, so macabre. Exhilarating.

So the morning of the 6th, when Maynard said he was taking his coach to the Bonny to witness the capture of the two men who had stolen twenty-four barrels of whale oil from his warehouse—a considerable sum of money, he told her—she begged him to bring her. She had recently found out she was with child, and knew that once she began to show, Maynard would not permit her to leave the house. Too delicate, he'd tell her.

But she was glad he'd brought her, because the Bonny was everything she'd hoped and more. The little Black child in chains; the angry, diminutive man preaching from the soapbox; the seemingly mystical woman in green; the gaggle of hogs amongst drunks; and, of course, the sudden arrival of the pigeons obscuring the sky. A day to remember, she planned to write in her diary.

"There," her husband screamed amongst the gunfire raining down birds upon them. "They will have them now!"

Two men ran from the livery, a pale man slipping into the mud, and a bronze man so beautiful he looked like a sculpture, she thought.

Three men in dark suits followed. Rifles raised.

"My Pinkertons," Maynard said. "For the money I have spent, they should put those men down quick."

Her husband was nearly frothing at the hunt, just like during the war when he had served as a colonel. He missed it, he once confessed. He missed the kill.

Then more shots fired, close enough to startle her. Mary shut her eyes, prayed. For how long, she never could remember.

Because when she opened her eyes, the street changed, shifted. She felt it but couldn't yet see why, until her husband grasped his pistol, stepped into the street. Three men, including the preacher, stood over the Black child, now dead.

Two Black men tried to intercede, holding up their spades to fight the killers, but before they could reach the boy, Maynard shot them down.

"The boy slayed a white man," Maynard said.

Chapter Twenty-Seven

She turned toward the two thieves, saw the pale one on his knees, before Maynard fired another shot into his chest. Meanwhile, the beautiful man fought off the Pinkertons with his sword. He was valiant in battle, a romantic, swashbuckling hero in the Byronic vein, Mary thought.

"We must get you to safety," Maynard said. He opened a door to a tavern and told her to remain downstairs until he came for her.

"Will you not join me?"

But there was a glee about him, a disposition of joy. "No, I must protect the city from the Negro uprising."

Uprising? It did not seem that way to her, but she wouldn't question him, not in public. When he shut the door behind her, she walked carefully down the stairs. She had never been in a tavern, did not know what to expect.

What she found was something old, ragged, and smelly. And also something quite sad. At the bar sat a lone woman, several months with child. Weeping.

"Dear, what is the trouble?" Mary asked.

The woman raised her head. She was quite plain to look at, but not dirty. This was no harlot.

"Here," Mary said, handing her a kerchief. "Let me help you."

CHAPTER TWENTY-EIGHT

<u>October 27, 1929—Port Kydd, USA</u>

...On his first day on Flywell Island, Joshua listened to the water lap lightly against the shore like a brush against canvas. He imagined the islands off the coast of California and saw him and Lily and their daughter sitting on the shore with a picnic. He'd teach their daughter how to fish. Her skin would be freckled, a bit sun bleached, and, in his mind, she smelled like strawberries...

...He opened his eyes to a man in a trench coat bent over the toilet, vomiting blood. Joshua looked closer. The coat was Army issued, brown with copper buttons, and his face had a stretch of scar from ear to chin. A scrape with a blowtorch. There were two-dozen other men in the cell, half of them veterans, some missing limbs, while others just leaned against the wall with crossed arms, feigning sleep. A Black man in Navy blues sat cross-legged, humming to himself. An Italian-looking vet threw a baseball against the stone. When it bounced back to him, he dropped it half the time on account of his missing left eye. "Figures," he said. "Fuckin' figures." Another man, this one scrawny and tattooed from neck to waist, wore just a towel and sang "Over There" until someone told him to shut it.

The stench of dead seabirds and diesel exhaust slunk through the window and came to a rest in the mortar. The men who had been there the longest owned the corners, sleeping under coats they'd stolen from dead prisoners. The thicker coats kept the stench away. The thickest even kept the rats from finding you. Joshua eyed a consumptive near the bars who looked like he had only a few hours left. His jacket was made of lambskin but frayed at the elbows. Good enough, Joshua thought, and he was willing to fight for it. His right hand quivered and he had to hide it in his pocket from the others. No one talked to him…

…On the second day, he awoke in the consumptive's coat, while a guard choked the Italian vet with his nightstick. The vet held onto the ball for what felt like a minute—but had to be less—before finally letting go. Joshua reached for the ball but both of his hands shook so violently that he couldn't squeeze them shut. Later, the guards made Joshua and the tattooed vet carry the body out to potter's field.

That night Miss Amand came to him in a dream. Or a vision. He wasn't sure. She walked him through the Swill, pointing out the new mementos they'd hung on the wall since he'd been away: Rafael's saber, Lily's camera, Olive's paint brush, a newspaper clipping of an Irish President who'd been shot, a tiny film screen that you could turn off and on with a button, an electric bilge pump to keep the rising Crabbe at bay. He awoke crying in the dark. Nearby an old man tried to masturbate, while the tattooed vet hung from the bars, his towel the noose…

…On the third day, Joshua was released.

"Why?" he asked. He stood naked in the jail yard—his face, head, and genitals shaved—while a guard hosed away the lice and bed bugs. His jaw trilled from Duffy's blackjacking and when the water stream hit him, train brakes echoed through his skull.

"Don't know," the guard said. "Word was you weren't ever leaving."

It was late when he got back to the Swill. He stood outside of the front door with his hands in his pockets and listened to longshoremen loading ships and women laughing down Pirate's Alley and a dog barking from a nearby apartment. He itched. He scratched his arms raw. Was she still inside? Had she gone to stay with her parents? If she were home, how would she look at him with his shaved head and the blue bruise lighting up his jaw? The last time they'd really spoken, she'd made him feel weak. Duffy's blackjack fortified that feeling. It had been a long three days of thinking.

He didn't have a key so when he pulled the handle he expected it to be locked but it opened up. He went downstairs and found Lily sweeping up glass, her hair tied in a kerchief. He paused on the landing, standing before the portrait of the old Revolutionary, watching her sweep and he held his breath, waiting for her to look up. When she finally did, she dropped the broom and brought her hands to her face.

"Oh, Rivers," she said, "it looks like a horse kicked you."

CHAPTER TWENTY-NINE

She drew a bath and slathered a salve across his jaw and then poured a double bourbon just to be safe. She helped him out of his clothes, took a sniff, and then put them in the garbage. She apologized for not having ice—there hadn't been a delivery. When Joshua slunk into the tub his shaking hands splashed water onto the tile floor. She reached over the brim and dunked his hands, hoping to calm them, and when that didn't work, she made him take the whiskey and then poured another. He kept crying.

"We'll get through this," she said. "I promise."

He shut his eyes, thought about digging a grave, lowering the Italian man inside; the man's head slunk to the side in a way that wasn't natural.

"What are you thinking about?" she said.

He'd held up the tattooed vet's legs when the guards cut him down.

"Rivers?"

He couldn't tell her any of this because she'd know how scared he was.

"When I was inside—" He paused, startled at the sound of Orla coming in. His chest felt like it was splitting open. Calm down. Tell her a joke.

"What? What did they do to you?"

"Nothing, nothing, nothing like that," he said. "But when I was inside I had a dream that you'd run off, that you'd gone and found yourself a stockbroker, you know someone with a top hat for every day of the week and that you had little stockbroker babies and they all got fitted for little tuxedos."

"How did I look?"

"Good, except you were smoking through a cigarette holder. Seemed wrong."

"Ha, look at this," she said, showing him the paper.

His wet hand sopped up the ink as he skimmed the front page describing the market crash. It was the first he'd heard of it. Men who'd been kings of the city now eyed the pavement from twenty stories up. In a speech before the Chamber of Commerce, Jasper Smythe said, "This is no time for the weak to lead. We must be brave in the face of this minor misfortune. Capital remains strong." The writer, however, noted that "Mr. Smythe appeared somewhat rattled during his speech. His voice lacked the usual vigor we have come to expect from him." The Bonny, however, hadn't looked a lick different because there were no banks in the neighborhood, just loan sharks. Still, Joshua thought, when someone like Jasper was hurting, it was only a matter of time before someone like Joshua felt his boot heel.

"And even if it weren't the case, I'd never trade you in for a stockbroker," Lily said. She rung out the sponge and then rubbed it along his shoulders. "A doctor, maybe. My mother would swoon."

"A lawyer. You like crooks."

"We've all got types."

He thought about Neal, wondered if he'd been with her when she found out about the arrest, if he'd stayed to comfort her, but she was being too nice to start a fight, and he was much too beaten up to win one. So he asked what the last three days had been like, if anyone had come by to help.

"Crickets," she said. "I mean, that cop Duffy stopped in to apologize. Brought a casserole and a dog bone."

"A dog bone?"

"Orla bit him after he arrested you. Otherwise, it's been just Rafael and me. Not even your sister, the bitch."

There'd been no word from Smythe or Vanderhock but she still felt their presence. She'd gone looking for a lawyer, but she either got kicked out straightaway or told to find another husband because hers wasn't coming home. Even the lawyers up in the Jewish Quarter and down on Graaf Street were too afraid of Jasper Smythe to help her. Rafael had no more luck. He'd asked around the neighborhood, talking to some local toughs about what they knew, but they all told him the same thing— the Riverses will get no help. Even Miss Amand stopped coming around. Abandoned, Lily said.

"The damn cowards," she said. "I thought they were our friends."

He could hear a change in her voice, a bitter quiver. Something had broken in the time he'd been away, some sort of faith Lily had in Port Kydd, in the neighborhood. There was no way she could have known whether or not Joshua was ever coming home, and the people who shared her street had left her to mourn alone. It was a betrayal, one she couldn't forgive.

"I hate everyone," she said. "When things got tough, every last one of them hid under the bed."

He thought about this as she got him into pajamas and then to bed. She shut the lights and sat beside him, looking out the window. Underneath all the violence, she'd believed Port Kydd was inherently good, that it protected its own, that one or two men couldn't simply usurp justice because of an old grudge. He'd *never* believed that and the differences in their upbringings—the boy from the Bonny and the girl from the Jewish Quarter—were now as stark as they'd ever been. He'd been raised on stories of the Bonny's betrayals, on the race riot that nearly burned down the neighborhood, of all the unjust killings. It was a story no one talked about, except for his grandmother. Everyone else chose to forget or to say it wasn't a big deal. Lilly was right. They were a neighborhood of cowards. He shut his eyes. For three days, he'd leaned against jail bars, so he'd expected to pass out, but when that didn't happen, he asked Lily what she wanted to do.

She looked toward the apartments across the street, at neighbors who no longer spoke to her.

"Run," she said.

"What?" Joshua sat up in bed. It hurt. "You don't mean it."

"No, I do. Rivers, I've had a lot of time over the last few days to think about our future. And I came to the same answer, whether or not you got out. We have to leave. You were right. I don't know where, but we need to go. We'll have Rafael watch the joint until we sell."

"What about the baby?"

"You know they have doctors outside of Port Kydd, right? We'll be fine as long as we get away from these bastards. They can't catch us if they don't know where we are."

He wanted to bring up all the reasons she had wanted to stay, but he was so relieved by the thought of leaving, of being on a train west, of seeing long open plains and a horizon that stretched to heaven that he simply said, "I've got a place in mind."

He shut his eyes and felt the first tremors of sleep but right before it took hold, he sat up with a start.

Who got him out of jail?

CHAPTER THIRTY

He awoke ready to fight, throwing closed fists at the air. Orla jumped off the bed and disappeared into the closet. He waited for the pain and when it showed, he grabbed the bedding and ground his teeth. He took a moment, breathed in the bedroom air, sensed Lily's perfume, the soap on the sheets, the aroma from Styer's Bakery. By the sound of the street—the paperboy calls, the busted shocks of the crosstown trolley, the clamber of bottles being collected—he knew it was probably mid-morning, but there was hardly any light coming through the window so it felt like dawn. This side of the building didn't see the sun much during the autumn. Meanwhile, Lily hunched over the bureau, sorting through clothes. In her paisley housedress, she picked up a piece of her wardrobe, held it to the light, and then put it in a pile: one for keeping, one for throwing out, and another for second thoughts.

"Hi," he said. His voice was scratchy, dry. He reached for a cigarette.

"What's the weather like in this place?"

"What?" He coughed and then took a drink of water.

Chapter Thirty

"The weather, Rivers. The weather. What should I bring? How should I dress? Do I need galoshes? Mittens? An evening gown?"

She turned around holding a black wool coat. She'd worn it the day he asked her to marry him. It had been snowing and he'd tried to take her to a French joint over in Cooke Village, but the snow had shut down the trains and she'd worn bad shoes. He'd thought of waiting until their next dinner but the ring was weighing down his pocket, so he proposed at the bottom of the Swill's stairs.

"Rivers? You there? We're still going, right?"

"Yeah, yeah, we are," he said. "It's nice most of the time."

"More specific, darling. What do you mean by nice?"

"You'll need a sweater at night. Some good walking shoes. An umbrella once in a while."

"And in the winter?"

"That is the winter. The summer is a lot like that too but it doesn't rain."

She gave him a hard glance.

"Is your head okay?" she asked.

"No, but that doesn't mean I'm wrong about the weather."

"Maybe. Are there a lot of bugs?"

He smiled. "Hardly any. An occasional spider or rattlesnake but nothing like the roaches we got here. Hell, you could go a month without seeing a mosquito."

"Hmm."

She didn't believe him or anyone else when they talked about California. People from Port Kydd thought it was a racket.

She went back to her sorting, holding up a sleek black dress, one she wouldn't need, and then put it in the "second thoughts" pile. There was far too much in the "yes" but he didn't want to give her a reason to change her mind.

"We'll keep some of it with your parents," he said. "They can send it out later."

"My parents, Christ. What am I going to tell my parents? They're getting that grandchild they've dreamed about since Warsaw and I'm up and leaving for California a week before I deliver?"

He sighed, thought about it for a second, and then said, "Maybe they should come when it feels safe."

"Have you met them? They can't handle being away from the city. They can't handle country accents. They barely talk to you."

"They don't speak in country accents in California. Besides, they like the pictures. Tell them I got a job in Hollywood."

She hesitated, then said, "Money. What are we going to do about money?"

"I've got a pile of cash under the bar. Remember? And we'll get something for this place."

"Unless your crazy sister wants it."

He lowered his eyes. "I wouldn't count on that."

"Are you going to go see her? "

"I don't know."

"You don't owe her anything."

He limped over to the closet for his robe. Orla was lying beside another open suitcase full of picture frames of Lily's parents and sister, two cameras, and a bundle of baby clothes. He crouched and scratched Orla behind the ears.

"And you little one," he whispered. "What are we going to do with you?"

"We're bringing the damn dog," Lily called out.

"I guess I have my answer."

CHAPTER THIRTY-ONE

After he worked a razor around his jaw and guzzled some coffee, he set out wearing a coat and tie, carrying a bag full of junk to sell, some money to pay back debts, and the intention to say goodbye to old friends. If he was leaving, he was doing it the right way, rather than setting out with a day's notice like he had at sixteen.

The newsstands were full of dire headlines, warnings of shutdown factories, of men out of work, of the stock crash rolling its way down his street. He thought about what he would miss about the Bonny and it was this: the raw life of the street, the pushing and shoving of cultures, stirred into this neighborhood stew. He felt nostalgia creeping in and it worsened when he spotted familiar faces but that quickly disappeared when they saw him and turned away. He thought at first they didn't recognize him. His bruised jaw and shaved head might have disguised him. But, no, he looked them right in the eye and though they tried to hide it, a wave of recognition—then fear—passed over their faces. They knew exactly who he was and they wanted no part of him. George McDonald, the plumber, walked by Joshua without so much as a nod. Daniel Bennett, who slept at the Swill when he was just off the boat from Liverpool, saw Joshua coming and crossed the street to avoid him. Even Hattie Davis, who Joshua lent money to after she'd left her husband, ducked into Tommy Cringle's tavern just to avoid sharing the same sidewalk.

He was being cut out. Erased.

He'd seen it before, when Lottie Franks started going with a gangster from Little Holland and her father put out word that she wasn't to be treated as family anymore, when Joe Pissarro started whispering to cops, and when Leo O'Malley beat his wife into a coma. It was a way to keep order in the neighborhood. Yet Joshua hadn't done any harm to these people as far as he could tell. He'd just defended his sister and in doing so, he'd pissed off the wrong guys. Nothing more.

His first stop was St. Nicholas' Pawnshop, a coal-stained storefront off of Bonny Lane. It had been here for decades, back when the owner, Big Vincent, used to buy Nellie's tavern-found treasures. When the old man died a few years back, his grandson Little Vincent, a light pole of a kid, took over. When Joshua stepped inside the shop, dust fell through a stream of sunlight, spotlighting a cornucopia of tossed-off junk, from saddles to ladies' pistols, wedding bands to belt buckles, while Little Vincent sat behind the counter reading the paper.

"Hey Vin, I've got some watches and a couple of hats left behind at the Swill," Joshua said. "There's also a decent bracelet in here and a couple of wallets."

Little Vincent turned around to look at the register.

"I'm leaving town, so I'm looking for some travel money."

Joshua reached over the counter and tugged at Little Vincent's sleeve. Nothing. Instead, Little Vincent walked to the back office and shut the door.

"Friendship, history," Joshua said. "Don't they mean anything to you?"

Chapter Thirty-One

The Averys were no better. Down at their Alvel Street ware-house, amidst barrels of beer, Joanna Avery saw Joshua and said, "Beat it."

"Look, I'm blowing town, just wanted to pay what I owed."

Joanna crossed her arms.

"I was helping my sister. That's it."

"They'll torch this place. Vanderhock, Smythe. You've made a mess."

"You're scared of them? I thought you had more mettle than that."

"Get the hell out. Get the hell out and never come back."

Even the Styers turned on him. Old Ginny Styer, stooped over an accounting book, pencil in her mouth, glanced up when Joshua came in and then cried, "No."

"I'm just here because I owe you money and Lily and I are leaving town."

"You got to go," she said.

Her son Charlie came out of the back wearing an apron cov-ered in flour. He picked up a rolling pin and smacked it against his free hand.

"What did I ever do to you?"

"Fucking Riverses," he said. "Every last one of you thinks you're so fucking smart and you're always getting yourself shat on, you fucking dolts. Fuck off and get the fuck out."

So he got the fuck out. He stood in front of the bakery as people stepped off the sidewalk to avoid him. He was dead to even Miss Amand. Outside John McArthur's tavern, she stood wearing a man's green suit, with a cigar and a mug. He waved but her eyes arched over him, landing somewhere down the street.

What could he expect from these people, these scared folks? They'd always been like this, and he'd been one of them, no more than the dirt under powerful men's feet. Yeah, the Bonny could kick the weak, the scared, the Black. But when he'd pushed back against someone tougher, they let him hang. Maybe that was Olive's point. The values he'd held, the loyalty he had to his neighbors, was never going to be matched. The Riverses were part of the Bonny but still separate. And maybe loving the Bonny hadn't been worth it? What had the neighborhood done for anyone except kill the young?

Across the street, the Swill's old brick was chipped and stained with bird shit and he couldn't imagine anyone ever thinking it was beautiful. His grandmother's painting had turned it into a sort of gold, so that it loomed like a palace. What made her see it that way? What made her see this street, this neighborhood as worth her time? Her lover was shot right in front of her. A dozen men were murdered afterward, including that Black child. And Rafael had been nearly killed for not looking Irish. Yet that painting made it all look beautiful.

Usually, in this kind of mood, he'd have gone and got a drink, but no one was going to sell him a bottle so he went home because there were three shelves full of booze needing to be emptied. The door was unlocked and when he came downstairs he called for Lily, but all he saw was that photographer friend of hers, Neal, slouched at the bar, reading a book, and drinking Tanqueray. Joshua had gotten a couple of bottles from Roche over the summer but no one had been interested in paying what it was worth, so they just sat there getting dusty. It was remarkable little Vanderhock hadn't broken them too, but they'd been too high up for such a short kid.

"That stuff's not cheap," Joshua said.

Neal pointed at a twenty on the bar. The man passed out money like he printed it in his basement.

"Gin isn't for collecting," Neal said. "Have some. My treat."

My treat? The ass. Still, Joshua poured one and when Neal raised his glass, Joshua, despite everything in his body telling him to kick the guy out, clinked it.

"To new beginnings," Neal said.

Joshua took the whole of the glass and then poured a second. "Where's Lily?"

"Said she had to see her mom," Neal said. "Tell her you're leaving town."

"Those people are going to hate me even more than they already do."

"She said that too." Neal closed his book. It was the same novel the Stranger had been reading six months earlier. *Red Harvest.*

"You found your father," Joshua said.

"I did. Gave me this. Gave me a handshake. Went on his way."

Neal flipped through the pages and then put it down. "Not my taste. So you did know him?"

"Didn't give me a name, but I figured you two might be related."

"He say anything about me?" Neal said.

"Said you were full of stupid at times."

"Ha. He would."

"Also told me a story about back when my grandmother ran this place," Joshua said. "It was a good story."

"Do you think it was true?"

"Does your dad lie a lot?"

"Yeah. He's pretty good at it too."

At the time, Joshua had thought it had made him love this place even more, but now, thinking it over, thinking about how Rafael had nearly gutted a man, he wasn't so sure how to feel.

"I don't know if it was true. It sounded right," Joshua said. "So that's why you came by, to tell me that?"

"No, it's because I want you to know I'm not in love with your wife. It was just a passing thing. I just don't have a lot of people who will sit and listen to me anymore. Didn't mean to cause you any worry if that's what you've been worried about."

Joshua lit a cigarette.

"California. That's a good place to run to." Neal's voice got a bit excited, or maybe it was just the booze setting in. "You can be entirely new out there. That's what people told me though I still kept calling myself Neal for some reason, living the same way I've always lived. I should have changed it to Arthur. Seems like a strong name."

"My grandfather's name was Jude," Joshua said. "Always liked that."

Neal's eyes settled on the piano. "I love old taverns. It's a shame this place is going by the wayside."

"You want to buy it? It's yours."

Neal paused, thinking, before laughing. "I'd be dead in a month. I've always relied on bartenders to throw me out and save my life. If I was the bartender, who would save me?"

Joshua brought the drink to his lips before putting it down. "You just learn to drink slowly," he said. He glanced at Neal's camera bag.

"What is it?" Neal asked.

"I was wondering, I mean, don't answer it unless you want to and I don't like to talk about it myself but I was wondering, well, what was your war like? You took pictures. Just can't see myself being there without a gun."

"Nice way of saying it. Most guys just call me a 'pansy.' The truth is, I was excited by it at first. Then, after I saw more dead bodies than I could photograph, I started feeling a lot of shame, regret, that sort of thing. Then I felt nothing at all. I'd come across a bunch of men gas dead, take a picture, and then sell it. Like I was putting together a car inside Ford's factory. One

Chapter Thirty-One

severed leg here, one bullet through the head over there. Just work. Eventually, I ran away. What was your war like?"

"Still running, aren't I?"

Neal raised his glass again. "Cheers to that."

CHAPTER THIRTY-TWO

The next morning, the phone woke Joshua. He reached for Lily but instead found a note saying she'd gone to the doctor. He wrapped the pillow over his ear but the phone kept ringing and when he couldn't fall back to sleep, he got up, groaning, the pain starting in his chin and working its way down, and went out to the hall and picked up the receiver. It was Duffy.

"Go to hell."

"Sorry. Hit you harder than I meant to," Duffy said. "Habit, I guess."

"Can this wait?" Joshua said.

"I know you're just putting the joint back together, but you mind making a trip uptown? Smythe wants to see you at the library. Know it's not great timing but I think you'll want to see this."

"And if I don't?"

"I'll have to have two of my not-so-bright boys give you a ride up here, so just leave your gun at home and make nice, will you?"

He'd seen Duffy's not-so-bright boys so he took a cab up to the library. At the front entrance, Hess waited in a white suit and dark glasses.

"A very nice bruise," he said, pointing at Joshua's jaw. "I imagine your woman is disappointed at the state of your profile."

"Why hasn't anyone killed you yet?"

Hess looked out at the passing of traffic. "I am very good."

He led Joshua to the back of the library and then into a dark stairwell, while the Austrian's gun jiggled under his coat. Joshua thought about how long it would take to get out of town. He'd have to square things with Rafael and Olive. But he couldn't wait too long. If Lily had the baby before they left, they'd be marooned in the city for weeks. He didn't know much about kids, but he figured you couldn't just board a train with a newborn and expect everything to be fine. Hess' gun made him think these things because he was scared the Austrian would put one in him before he got a chance to get free of this whole mess.

Hess seemed to sense this fear. "Mr. Rivers. We wouldn't have called you here for murder. Come."

When they got to the basement, Duffy, Jasper, and the librarian Raab were perched over the table, each holding a magnifying glass.

"Mr. Rivers," Raab started, "what happened to your face and your hair?"

Joshua rubbed his shaved scalp and looked at Duffy. "Lice."

"Yeah, it's something else out there," Duffy said.

Jasper didn't seem to be up for talking. He looked shaken, mumbling something too quiet for Joshua to hear.

Duffy pointed at the table. "Come here and tell us what do you make of this because it's about the damnedest thing I've run into on the job."

Joshua saw what they were riled up about. On the table, spread out and flattened by paper weights, lay four exact copies of *The Passenger Pigeons*. Each was the same size and looked exactly like its brother, from the bronze sky to the Black child. Even his grandmother's signature was exact.

"How the hell—?"

"That's what we were hoping you could answer," Raab said.

Joshua turned to Jasper in his ill-fitting suit and saw that the rich man was tired. The stock crash, the papers said, hit his company especially hard and no matter how much he told the public that everything would turn out fine, Joshua could see that wasn't the case. Everything Jasper thought about himself was slipping away. It made Joshua smile.

"What is she doing?" Jasper asked.

"How would I know?" Joshua said. "You know where I've been."

Joshua turned to Raab. The librarian ran his finger along the edge of his mustache and then checked the time. He seemed amused.

"They're the same size?" Joshua asked.

"As far as I can tell," Raab said. "I need to examine them further but I can hardly see a difference. Whoever did these was sitting in the right light and the brush strokes, it's, well, identical. They don't even make brushes like this anymore. The hair is very specific."

"The other pictures that were stolen," Joshua said. "Were they also the same size?"

"Close enough that a cut here and there would do it," Raab said. "Do you think your sister could have painted over them? That would be a tragedy."

"I don't know that she stole them."

Jasper shook Joshua with a weak, desperate sort of jerk, the kind a spoiled kid gives when you take away his chocolate. Or a rich man scared of hard work. "Why is she doing this?"

Joshua pushed Jasper against the table. Hess smiled. Joshua turned to Duffy. "Where'd you find these?"

"That's the queer thing," Duffy said. "Got a call yesterday, gave me some rich people's names, and there in their living rooms, over the mantles, I found these."

"How do we figure out which is the right one?" Jasper said.

"They might all be the right one," Raab said. "Mr. Rivers is right. She may have painted over three of them or perhaps none of them are. Perhaps they're all forgeries. If that's the case, then your paintings are still missing. The insurance company, however, is going to have some questions."

Jasper looked sapped. More than ever, he needed that insurance payout, Joshua figured. And if it ever came out that he'd hired Olive, his chances of becoming the Mayor were done for. Is that what Olive wanted? Joshua looked again at the paintings. He wasn't sure what the hell Olive was up to, but he knew, at the very least, this wasn't just over money.

It was then that Raab snapped his fingers. "The hospital," he said. "We can do it there."

"Are you speaking in riddles you fat fool?" Jasper said.

Raab took a deep breath before explaining that if you put a suspected forgery under an X-ray, you could sometimes see if another painting was beneath it, one invisible to the naked eye. Forgers often painted over old paintings, so that the paper itself was the right age.

"I suspect the correct one will be the only painting without a second beneath it. We'll also know if these were painted over Nellie Rivers' other works. Dear, God, I hope not."

Joshua remembered the picture Vanderhock had shown him of his broken thumb six months earlier. He wondered if Olive knew this. He suspected she did.

"Detective Duffy," Jasper said. "Will you talk some sense into Mr. Rivers. Let him know how the world works."

Chapter Thirty-Two

"Of course, sir," Duffy said.

Duffy walked Joshua outside and stopped beside the marble elephants.

"Is this when you talk some sense into me?" Joshua said.

Duffy spit. "I've got five murders on my desk, a dozen muggings, and some guy who set his kid on fire but I've spent the last week chasing these damn things. Sorry about the jaw again."

"Sorry my dog bit you."

"Good dog."

"She is. Hey, do you know who bailed me out?"

Duffy didn't. Said it was done in the middle of the night. A man came in with a briefcase full of cash for the bail and probably some extra for the cops so no one asked too many questions. Joshua didn't know what to think.

"I wouldn't worry about that," Duffy said. "Listen, if I were you, I'd get out of town."

"Was thinking the same thing."

CHAPTER THIRTY-THREE

He couldn't find Olive alone, so he called Rafael and they started their search at the old Victorian on the edge of Little Holland where he'd seen Olive days earlier. It had the same rundown look as before but Joshua saw that the building didn't stand straight up and down but tilted just a bit to the east as if something invisible was weighing it down. Rafael waited outside the door grinning like a gambler who'd just dropped four aces. He held up the paper. There'd been some bank runs on Graaf Street and the rich were bleeding cash like someone had pierced their wallet's artery.

"The suffering of wealthy *Yanquis* brings me great pleasure," he said. "May they be vagabonds by Christmas."

"Glad I sold all my stocks," Joshua said, though he didn't feel right joking about it. Even if it was good to see Jasper hurting, he knew that pain got kicked downward. He said this but Rafael was too old to care.

"A touch of mayhem is good for the town's soul." He pointed at the building and then said, "Why are we at this pitiful abode?"

"I've got to see Olive," Joshua said. "Me and Lily are leaving town."

Joshua stepped into the cold entranceway. No one had been here in days, abandoned, he figured, as soon as she showed it to him.

"It appears as if someone took great care of this house for a time and then deserted it. One could say that about this entire neighborhood. Still, I feel something familiar, something I can't quite remember."

"A lot of these places look alike."

"What do you plan to do with the Swill?" Rafael said.

Joshua started up the stairs, calling out Olive's name.

"Joshua," Rafael said from the bottom of the stairs. His tone made Joshua turn. "The Swill. What will happen to her?"

"I don't know," Joshua said. "I'll see if Olive wants her."

"She will not."

"Then sell it. Not much of a choice with us in California. You should come. You always talked of California like—"

"They will knock her down, turn her into some vile tenement."

"People need a place to live."

In the railroad apartment, Olive had left behind the two chairs, the bouquet of dead roses, and the giant rat in the fireplace.

Rafael knocked it with the fire poker. "Someone skinned this Crabbe Rat."

"Crabbe Rat? Can't be. They're extinct."

"Not quite. You still seem them on a full moon by the shore. What is that odor?"

Below the vase Joshua found a small dish with a rose-colored stain inside it.

"Blood?" Rafael asked.

Joshua lifted the dish to his nose.

"Paint. She wanted the Crabbe rat's hair," Joshua said. "For the paint brush, so it looked right."

"Clever girl," Rafael said. "Almost as clever as the first man I ever killed."

Before Joshua could ask what was wrong, Rafael was already heading downstairs. It was no matter. Joshua saw what Olive was showing him. He looked up to the window, at the light. The shadows would have been right.

"Come," Rafael called out.

In the basement, amidst empty milk crates, a wet draft seemed to cut through the wall. It smelled of sea air at low tide. Rafael pointed at an oval wall panel that looked like it had been pried open and then shut again.

"Do you believe your sister was this damned clever?"

"Something wrong?"

Rafael took his knife to the panel and popped it out and a rush of stale ocean air blew out. "Yes," Rafael said. "A clever girl, she is."

"You know what this is?"

Rafael ducked in with Joshua following slowly down a soft, grizzled staircase that led into the dark. Each step sounded like it would give and he'd plunge into the dark below. He expected to arrive at a tunnel like the one under the Swill, but it was just a small room with some moth-bitten clothes atop a pastor's lectern sitting in six inches of dark water.

"What is this?" Joshua said. He found a Bible atop a shelf.

"You are the genius of the family, I've always understood."

"What do you know that I don't?"

"Enough to write a book far too long for you to bother reading."

Joshua picked up one of the jackets. It was ragged with stiff, scratchy fabric, homespun, from the last century. There was a minister's collar pinned to it. He trudged around the room, holding his lighter, his boots soaked through. The room was built in an egg shape, with uneven walls made of mortar and river stone. The rafters looked like the Swill's, built sometime before the Civil War.

"What's going on here?" Joshua asked.

"This basement was built before the rest of the building and then they built on top of it decades ago, burying it," Rafael said. "There are a number of places like this in town. Older underground. Hidden rooms. This is the point of your sister's clever exercise."

Rafael pointed his lighter toward the wall, illuminating words written in what seemed like an ancient hand.

God has abandoned me
May the lord strike down upon the heathen head of my brother
To hell I shall venture for all life thereafter death
Thou is to swim into the darkness of Heaven
The Negro is the creation of the heathen god
I am the knight of the New Rotterdam

"Clever damn girl."

"What is this?"

"The elder Vanderhock lived here. One of the men who shot dead your grandfather."

"How do you know?"

"Because this is where I took *Collette* and struck him down. Vengeance for your grandfather's life, for your grandmother's sorrow. For the riot that nearly had me quartered."

Rafael turned and Joshua stepped back. The old man's gaze was as cold as any he'd seen in the War.

"I wish to buy the Swill."

"What? Why would you want that? You should come with us, come back to your home."

"I have been helping keep that tavern alive for over fifty years. Do you understand? I won't allow her to be turned to scrap because your dear mother left behind two dim children when she should have known better. Do you understand? Must I speak slower?"

Joshua had never been scared of Rafael before, but in the dark of the old basement, he understood why he should be. "I'll have to talk to Olive first."

"You do that. You do that quickly."

CHAPTER THIRTY-FOUR

Joshua returned to Mags' Hangout. Behind the bar, Mags reached for her brass knuckles, while, nearby, Olive's blonde sat sidesaddle on a bench. Her name was Joanie, he remembered.

"I need you to take me to her," he said.

"What if I ain't in the taking mood? You think of that big shot?"

He threw a ten on her lap. "Don't even have to suck my prick."

"You ain't as mean as her," she said, smoothing out the bill and holding it to the light. "But you're close."

Joanie made him pay for a cab. During the drive she slouched against the window, biting her nails, humming to herself.

"Where's your family?" he asked.

"How should I know?"

The cab stopped outside of a Cooke Village townhouse that was two stories of husked paint and five decades of neglect. There was a knocker in the shape of an owl and a pair of old women knitting on the next stoop over. They refused to look at him.

"Thanks," Joshua said, handing Joanie another dollar.

Chapter Thirty-Four

"You Rivers ain't worth the trouble." She tried to spit on his coat, but it just dribbled down her chin. "Better off on my own dime."

Inside he was greeted by walls papered in cherubs, surrounding a tattered fainting couch, all set under a high ceiling. This, he figured, was the room where they held parties back in the day. There was a chandelier wired for gas, which, despite the tarnish, was so beautiful Joshua could imagine Greta Garbo dancing beneath it. He ducked into a hall with a low ceiling and then found the stairs.

"Olive," he called out. "It's Joshua."

He didn't want to startle her. There was no telling how long she'd been sitting in the dark, holding a gun. So with each step he slammed his boots and called out her name, but there was nothing but mice crittering into their cracks. On the second floor, there was a long hall of bedroom doors and down at the end stood Molly, wearing a slip and pulling her dark hair into a ponytail.

"Think you woke the dead with that racket."

"Didn't want to surprise anyone," he said.

"Afraid I'd shoot you?"

"I don't give a fuck about you," he said. "Where is she?"

She thumbed toward the bedroom. "Should be nicer to me," she said. "We're practically family."

In the bedroom, Olive sat on a mattress on the floor, a bottle at her feet, and a pistol on her pillow. She wore the same slip as Molly. He stood there for a while, before she glanced at him.

"You look awful," Olive said. "The cops do that?"

He reached for his face, while a cat slipped around the corner and stopped beside Olive's leg.

"Four paintings?"

She smiled.

"Crabbe Rat hair?"

"Had to make them look right. You went back?"

"I did."

She nodded. "You look all over the house?"

"The basement, you mean?"

"Good boy, Joshua. Good boy. You know who wrote those words, don't you? You know where you were, right?"

"Rafael was with me."

"I imagine he's a bit angry. I get it. I think he still blames himself for Jude dying, but look this goes back years. Us, Smythe, Vanderhock. We're just playing out the string, you and me. Just the *people* doing what we always do, pushing back, keeping them in line."

He looked toward the window. "Lily and I are leaving Port Kydd, just came to tell you that. If you don't want the Swill, I'm going to sell her to Rafael."

She lit a new cigarette off the one she was already burning, then mashed out the old one hard enough to flip the ashtray. "Stop it. You're not going anywhere."

"You should go too. Let things die down."

"Do you ever get sick of hearing yourself?"

At the window he spied an alleyway draped with hanging linens and a woman leaning out a window, crying, on the other side of the line.

"How's this going to end? Have you figured that out?" he said.

"You haven't been paying attention. It doesn't end. Not with Smythe. I got no choice."

"Sure you do. You leave. Get a new life. Die old."

"This *is* it. Do you see what my life is?" she said. "Do you see all of it? Do you *hear* me? This is who I am."

"You don't have to be."

She got up and he could feel how sick of him she was in the way she moved across the room. She'd been holding it in a long time and when she looked back, he could tell she was done being polite.

"Is that what your bitch wife's been telling you?" she said. "That you've got a choice? That you don't have to end up like me? Or maybe she's worried your kid will?"

He stepped back. It had been at least twenty years since she'd raised her voice at him.

"Leave Lily out of this."

"I know what she's saying about me. That I'm no good, that I'm nuts, that there's something wrong with me."

At the window, she held her pistol casually, like a drink.

"I used to wonder what made you go and marry a girl like that but then I remembered it's your character, isn't it?" she said. "You always wanted it easy. It was too hard here, so you ran. It got hard out there all alone, so you ran back. One giant cowardly circle. Same with that wife of yours. Too afraid of a real girl, so you go and marry one without the sharp edges."

"She's plenty sharp enough."

"Ha fucking ha! She's as dull as a goddamn spoon. Just look at her. She dresses all pretty and takes pictures. How sweet. How utterly sweet and girlish. It's just like you to marry some dainty little princess rather than a girl who could push back. You never did like that about us Rivers girls. That we could give as good as you. It's because of her you've gone soft, admit it? Ten years ago you would have slit that little Vanderhock kid's throat. Now you're scared. Too scared to do what needs being done. He bats around your wife and you just take it."

It was another woman calling him soft, but this time he didn't have to take it. There were too many thoughts in his head to say any of them so he went to the door intent on never seeing her again. Sometimes even the people we love got to go down. This was one of those times.

"So you're just leaving?" she said. "Too hard?"

Chapter Thirty-Four

Silhouetted in the dusty window's light, she reminded him of their grandmother. The old woman would stand at her bedroom window, sometimes for hours at a time, looking out onto the street. He never knew what she was thinking about. He never asked.

"Olive," he said. "During the War, I—"

She was about to speak, but then there was a beat—shorter than a single breath—between the sight of the window breaking and Olive crashing to the floor.

The room went blue, then red. A hollow echo, nausea. On his knees, crawling, reaching for her. From the ground, pistol raised, she fired twice out the window. He shut his eyes. Ears burning. He got ahold of her by the thigh, dragging her toward the dark of the room. She shook him off.

"What are you doing?" she asked.

He found himself crawling toward the sill, peeking over. Below, on the concrete, a man lay dead, a gun nearby, while another man ran down the alley.

He recognized them. They'd both visited the Swill a few days earlier, accompanied by their boss, Joel Vanderhock.

Olive came up behind him. "Did I get him?"

CHAPTER THIRTY-FIVE

By the time Molly swept into the room, Joshua had wrapped Olive's arm in a torn shirtsleeve. The bleeding was steady but light, the bullet just nicking the skin. He cared for her arm in a rote, experienced way, wrapping it twice and tying it off without much thought, a sort of muscle memory learned in France. Molly crouched beside him, and then took Olive's hand and kissed it.

He went to the window, a dull sheen draping his eyes, palms soaked, heart doing double time. The man was still there, his gun waiting to be scavenged. But this wasn't the Bonny with her guttersnipes ready to pick from the dead. The cops would be here any moment.

Meanwhile, Olive was talking like she'd sucked down half the town's coffee.

"I can't believe I hit him," Olive said to Molly. "It was instinct, you know like how dogs know other dogs they hate. I just felt the fire in my shoulder and then I reached around and I only saw a shadow of him. You'd have been amazed. I knew I was a good shot but firing at a man is different except it isn't because you're not thinking but now I am."

Chapter Thirty-Five

Joshua knew what she meant but this wasn't the time to talk. "We have to go. We have to go now."

They ignored him.

"What were you thinking?" Molly asked.

"I'm thinking if he's got a wife she'll be relieved he won't be coming home."

Molly helped her up and Olive grunted and cried out a bit. "Jesus, oh Jesus. It hurts worse than you'd think. A lot worse."

He knew he had to leave town tonight, but there was one last thing he had to do because all of the people he loved didn't think he had it in him anymore. Because they'd slapped his wife and shot his sister. Be a man, he told himself.

"You okay, Joshua?" Olive asked.

"He's pissing himself," Molly said.

"Hey, my brother doesn't piss himself. He's a war hero. I showed you his medals."

A purple heart. A silver star. A victory medal. They were in a box somewhere in the attic. He'd sent them home after the War and forgotten all about them.

"The cops will be here any second," he said.

Olive made her way toward Joshua, a bit shaky on her feet. Adrenaline and blood loss, Joshua thought. She'd crash soon. At the window, she leaned against him, and then kissed him on the cheek. Whatever she'd said to him before had been forgotten with the first bullet.

"There," she said. In her hand was a snub-nosed revolver. "I've got another."

He pocketed it as the first sound of the siren flared down the road.

On the sidewalk, they looked for the second man but he was gone. Across the street, windows were open, eyes peeking, sketching his face into their memories.

"Go home, lay low," Olive said.

Chapter Thirty-Five

"Olive."

"I'll see you soon, big brother."

She took Molly's hand and pulled west, her ponytail bobbing up and down, just like when they were kids. This, he thought, was it for the Rivers siblings.

CHAPTER THIRTY-SIX

On the street, hat low, collar up, cigarette teeter-tottering on his lips. Don't run. Walk with purpose. Don't look at anyone. Don't look away. The sidewalk was bent, ribbed. Dark water pooled. He pushed past a pair of old women strolling a baby, and then stopped in front of a tailor's shop and looked at his reflection in the plate glass window. No one behind him. He moved on as waves of light crossed his eyes like a mirage. In the second-story windows he saw Germans with rifles. Inside the coats of old women he sensed grenades and gas masks. His left hand shook and he stuck it in his coat pocket next to the gun.

Get to Lily, get out of town.

Get to Lily, get out of town.

Get to Lily, get out of town.

But there was something else he had to do first. Olive said he couldn't do it. But he could. Had to. Just do it like you used to and then leave town.

By the time he reached Ansell Park he'd lost his hat and felt drenched in eyeballs. There was a boy in a yarmulke playing the violin. He swung the bow like a bayonet. Joshua wiped his forehead, while sweat pasted his shirt to his back. A dull pain finger-flicked his temples. He knew he was crying but there was nothing to do for that, like getting dust in the eye. He had to get away from people, get out of the crowd where someone could gut him and then disappear but he wasn't safe in any alley, one on one, no one to hear him scream. Keep moving. A car backfired. He pulled his gun and aimed at a streetcar rollicking past. Next to him a pair of women threw their purses at him.

"Sorry, sorry." He pushed on.

Hands shivered in his coat. Slalom around shoe peddlers and paperboys singing of Graaf Street bankers going broke. Keep to the edge of the sidewalk, right up against the shops. Need to have a good angle at the street, at anyone coming his way. Dive into a store at the first shot. A sweet smell, like blown dynamite, wafted past. In Raleigh Square, some out-of-work communists lolled in shirtsleeves while a drunk sang "Amazing Grace" to no one in particular. He stopped, made like he was listening and then bent down to tie his shoe. Take a breath. Don't go mad. Breathe. Keep your eyes open, just like the Sergeant said. Eyes open, he looked up. Vanderhock's tough was gazing right at him from across the park.

He ran, the echo of pounding boots behind him. He turned south down Logan. There was a deli up ahead and he dove into it and worked his way to the phone in the back. He dropped a nickel in, pulled his gun and aimed it at the counter. If anyone came in he'd be ready. He called home. Rafael picked up.

"I will find your wife," he said.

"No, wait. You got a gun on you?" Joshua asked.

"Did you hit your head? Of course."

"Lock the doors. Stay with Lily."

Joshua slipped out the back and down an alley, emerging onto Bonny Lane, moving slowly south, skirting the edge of the neighborhood. Eyes low, gun in his pocket, finger on the trigger. Light a cigarette. Look over your shoulder but don't look like you're looking over your shoulder. Stop at a bright window, look at the reflection but don't look like you're looking at the reflection. If he gets close, put the gun against his coat, pull the trigger, don't stop walking, hope the coat muffles the sound. Get on a train. Get a new name. Dye your hair silver. Don't stop. Not until you're on the other side of the country.

CHAPTER THIRTY-SEVEN

But there was one last thing.

Vanderhock's church was barely visible in the late dusk, the spire disappearing into the coal fog. Down here, they'd never replaced the old gas streetlights and the gasworks had shut down last year so walkers held out their hands, blind men afraid to bump into a street sign. This darkness made the light burning in the rectory all that much brighter. He crossed the street, climbed the fence, and then ran across the lawn toward the back of the church. He ducked beneath Vanderhock's window and pulled out his gun, hand shaking. Stop. Stop being scared. Be a man. His knee and jaw ached. The cold wind rustling against his bare scalp brought tears. He held his breath, listened. There was no sound from inside except the scribble of a pen.

He slipped around the corner toward the side entrance and at the door waited the kid with tortoiseshell glasses who'd been handing out mercy tracts a few months earlier. The boy bit on an unlit cigarette and seemed to be searching the sky for God but he wouldn't see him on a night like this. Joshua threw a rock at a neighboring window and when the boy turned Joshua pushed his gun against the boy's back and then took the boy's gun from his coat.

"You guys still friends?"

They walked through the dark hall, amidst the scent of burnt-out prayer candles. The boy knew not to talk. Vanderhock's door was open just enough to seep some light onto the hall floor. The boy bobbed his head toward the door, as if saying "it's your death sentence, chump." So be it. Joshua pushed the boy inside and onto Vanderhock's desk, scattering papers and nearly knocking a jug of wine onto the floor. Joel stood and reached into a drawer but thought better when he eyed Joshua's gun.

"Hand it over."

Joel slid an old double-barreled pistol across the desk, something from the Civil War. Joshua raised the muzzle for a sniff. It hadn't been fired in decades if ever at all. Joshua slipped it into his pocket next to the boy's.

"This isn't you, Rivers," Vanderhock said. "You're not this man."

"Tell that to all the German widows I made."

"You had a uniform on. This ain't sanctified by God or country."

Joel reached for his jug of wine and tipped it by his thumb and over his forearm, taking a gulp.

"Your boys took a shot at Olive."

"They did no such thing."

"I saw them. She popped one in the head." Joshua turned to the boy in the glasses. "You're in a tough profession. Thinking you might want to try something gentler, like selling encyclopedias."

The boy smirked.

"Wally and Fitz no longer work for me," Vanderhock said. "They took another offer, you could say. It has been a trying afternoon for us all. Come, Rivers, you're a better man than this. What do you think your grandmother would say, seeing you like this? How about your poor mother? Walking in here with a gun intending to murder me cold. Is that the boy those women raised?"

It was and Joshua said so.

"Cut it out. You're not Rafael Castillo or Jude Kelly," Joel said. "Look, I don't want any trouble from you."

"Then why do you keep bothering me?"

"I just want the painting. That's all."

There wasn't even a portrait of the Virgin Mary on the walls. "Who's it for?"

Joel wiped his glasses with his tie. "The fire. I want it to go in the fire, burned from history."

"Why? I've seen it. It's not doing Jesus any harm."

"That ridiculous little man," Joel said. "He was a black mark on my family's history."

"Your uncle?"

"Some Vanderhocks, well, are touched. Yes, God speaks to me but in symbols and metaphor."

"And shakedowns and protection rackets."

"To sin against a sinner is not a sin."

"Was that in the Book of Ruth?"

"You know what I mean," Joel said. "I see God's words in the works of history and in the way the sky lays down against the Earth. My uncle thought he had a direct line to the Lord. It told him to murder Negroes. They blame him for that. The history books. They say he started the Great Bonny Riot. That's what he did to my name. All those dead Negroes, right next to the once proud Vanderhock name. The paranoid little fool. But it's not just him. There's a strain of that in this city, in this country that's, well, troubling, a certain belief in conspiracy that I find maddening. And I don't want my name tied to it.

That painting does that. You can see the devil in his eyes and he looks just enough like me that I want it burned."

"It's too late," Joshua said. "Jasper has it."

Joel threw his Bible against the wall.

"He hasn't a right to it," Joel said. "Not a right."

Joel pointed at the boy. "Get a couple of the men together, you know which ones, and find Smythe's albino and bring him here. Don't be nice about it."

Joshua aimed at the boy but the kid just grinned out the door. Joel sat down and drained the rest of his wine.

"We owned them," Joel said. "We owned this whole Island and what do we get, a crumbling neighborhood and a congregation of crooks. Smythe. Damn Smythe. His daddy fired as many shots as my uncle and he gets to be king."

Joshua dropped Vanderhock's gun on his table along with the boy's. There was no point in going on with this ruse. Everyone was right. Whatever man he'd been in the War was long dead.

"Rivers, tell Olive to give me my money and we'll call it square. As for Smythe, well, that man will be mayor over my dead body and everyone else's in this neighborhood."

Joshua went to the door.

"And remember," Joel said. "I ain't the type to come after you unless I got a reason. I got pride but I ain't dumb. Smythe, though, he's both."

"Why do you care what he does to me?"

"I don't care if you lose, but I'll be damned if he wins."

CHAPTER THIRTY-EIGHT

A weak light slipped through the Swill's low windows and the front door was unlocked. No talk. No music. Joshua looked down the street, up at the second- and third-story windows, and searched for shadows moving inside of the dark storefronts. He leaned his head against the door, thoughts coming quick. *Run. Run. Run.*

But thinking did him no good so he opened the door and went down the stairs, gun at his side, before stopping beside Rafael who lay beneath the Revolutionary's portrait. The old man's hands were on his lap and he stared across the tavern.

There, behind the bar, Lily stood with her hands wrapped around her belly. A pistol muzzle stretched to a dark coat sleeve and up to the pale face of Hess. His shirt was covered in blood. There was a scratch along his throat, a bruising around his eye. Orla barked from inside the broom closet.

Joshua put his gun on the floor, raised his hands, and looked at the mirror behind the bar, reflecting the back of Lily's head, of Hess' head, and of his own reflection. He lowered his eyes.

"The old Mexican is a very able man, aren't you?" Hess said. "Very able."

Rafael kept quiet.

"How is your sister?" Hess said to Joshua. "I understand my men failed to kill her."

Hess' words floated in waves of blue. Orla kept barking. Joshua wanted to tell the dog to shut up.

"Escalation. You know this word? It is tactic they taught us in army. You begin with a threat, maybe insinuate harm upon brother. Then you find—what do you call—weakness. You send police for brother, and then wait and see if enough. Sadly, your sister escalates herself. Sends four paintings. So we escalate more. Mr. Smythe asks for her to die, so we send men to kill your sister, end this silly debacle. But they are not good men. I should have done work myself but Mr. Smythe insists I not bloody my own hands, but now that she lives and I can't find her so I must do what others cannot. So now we escalate again for there are worse ways to hurt a person than killing. It is circle. Escalation. Results. More escalation."

He ran his other hand through Lily's hair.

"It is just labor you see," he went on. "Part of occupation, of trade. I am employed to complete a task and I am paid very well by Mr. Smythe, but if your sister is not dead or jailed soon, there will not be any money for me from Mr. Smythe and then I must find Mr. Smythe's weakness. Circle. Mind me, I enjoy this work. There is pleasure in a job well done and Mr. Smythe has given me, what is phrase, 'carte blanche' to do job as I wish. He is not interested in the details, you see. Make a very bad mayor but good employer for a man like me. Your sister will be interested though. In details. I cannot imagine her wanting to keep up this silly game of hers if she is scraping dead child off floor."

Lily clenched her jaw until her face turned red.

"And I know you are just trying to aid your sister. A brother's duty. You did not want part of this fight between old families. I see that. But in order to escalate this so that we can come to agreement, I must cause your sister great pain, and you are her weakness, so I will cause you pain, humiliating, torturous pain. The sort your sister cannot match and cannot ignore. It is what they pay me for. To do what they themselves cannot do."

Rafael bowed his head.

"I am not going to ask you to speak. I cannot imagine how much hurt you feel now, the sort that will never leave. But you will let me know what you want. You have choice. Take your clothes off or scrape the floor."

Joshua undid his tie and threw it on the floor. He then took off his coat and his shirt and undershirt. Hess waved his gun. Joshua took off his shoes and trousers and socks leaving just his underwear and sock garters.

"Everything."

Joshua obeyed.

"Now put your hands on the table. Good. And you, you old Mexican move, we scrape the floor. Now lay your face on the table, Mr. Rivers. Just like that. Keep eyes open and look at your wife because after this you are going to want to kill your sister yourself and it will save me the bullet and you will probably put one in your head, which is how these moments sometimes end."

Hess slipped around Lily and came toward Joshua, who held fast to the table. Nearby, there was an old lamp he could use as a weapon, but there'd be a bullet in him before he reached it and then Hess would have to kill Rafael and Lily.

"Old Mexican move to bar."

Rafael moved to the bar.

"I am not an evil man, understand. Back in Vienna, I have a wife and four children and they believe I am an old silly soldier. They do not know that I work for Mr. Smythe. You see you cannot feed so many mouths on a soldier's pay. Keep your eyes open."

Chapter Thirty-Eight

Joshua looked at the bottles behind Lily. The gin shimmered like the ocean.

"There was boy at Verdun. An English boy, no more than sixteen I believe. He sang all the while under me, my hands on his back, and I think that helped him tolerate it, the suffering, the humiliation, the crowds cheering as I take him. He sang "The Lass that Loves a Sailor." I can still hear it. He went home in his brain, to see his lost love. And I told him it would be over soon and when I was finished he dressed and shook my hand and shook it and thanked me and then walked over to this ugly private and stepped into his bayonet. Do you believe so? He walked into it. And he did not ever understand that this is part of war, the humiliation. It is not as though I was treating him like prostitute, no. It was duty. As is this. This is escalation, a means to the end. Total victory."

He stepped behind Joshua and then unbuttoned his own trousers. It sounded difficult with one hand, so he laid his pistol on Joshua's back.

Lily appeared close to vomiting and then a calm came over her eyes, as if she realized this was just a picture show, a kind of make believe. Rafael lowered his head and Joshua was thankful for that, thankful he wouldn't look.

"There." Hess' trousers fell to the floor and his hand touched Joshua's back. "In Yorktown—"

His voice died from the first bullet. The rest followed with the second shot. He slipped down Joshua's back and onto the floor. Joshua opened his eyes as Lily came from around the bar with his army revolver and unloaded the rest of the bullets into Hess' face until there was nothing but a mess of pulp and offal.

PART FIVE: VETERANS OF FOREIGN WARS

CHAPTER THIRTY-NINE

December 6th, 1873

It had been Rafael's idea to go after Maynard Smythe. His long-time partner Jude Kelly thought it unwise.

"He owns half the city," Jude said.

"He destroyed my home," Rafael said.

This was true. Smythe was among a number of bankers who'd helped take over northern California during the Gold Rush, casting out rancheros like Rafael's family. At his birth, Rafael had been heir to a thousand acres of prime California grassland, nestled along the Russian River. And then the *yanquis* like Smythe brought legions of the most vile, greedy sorts—mostly southerners—to Rafael's home. The consequences were dire. His father died in prison, his mother of heartbreak, and his brothers of various ailments caused by grief and poverty, leaving Rafael as the only surviving Castillo, destined, Rafael believed, to wander the world seeking vengeance.

Rafael held up his saber, *Collette*, so that it glistened in Jude's eye.

"Stop it," Jude said.

"When Smythe is dead," Rafael said.

Chapter Thirty-Nine

They compromised on just stealing from the man. Jude had scouted a poorly protected warehouse full of whale oil, the cheap, necessary way to heat lamps.

"The stench," Rafael said.

"The money," Jude said.

Rafael trusted Jude. In fact, he loved Jude in the most noble platonic manner a gambler, thief, and whoremonger like Rafael could fathom. After all, Rafael believed that, without Jude, he would be dead. Six years earlier, Rafael was lost in the world, banished from California and wanted throughout most of continental Europe, when he found Jude in a Montreal brothel. *Le bouton de rose.* One of the lowliest houses Rafael had ever visited—unsophisticated company, lumpy mattresses, the odor of boiled potatoes seeping into the sheets. But in the parlor, he found Jude reading a copy of *Don Quixote* in the original Spanish, so the men went to a tavern where they discussed the beauty of Cervantes' masterpiece, while forging a bond over three bottles of a fine Spanish red.

Like Rafael, Jude has also been cast out from his home. He was an anarchist, believed in the ideals of communal agreement, the distribution of power to individuals, and the inherent corruption of both the English crown and the United States Republic. He was also an atheist, a position his family could not abide, they told him, as they pushed him out of his home. Jude's atheism bothered Rafael as well, since, as a royalist and a Catholic, he thought the dilution of power amongst the masses was the quickest route to hell.

"I'll convince you," Jude told him.

"Never."

For the next six years, Jude argued and Rafael mocked and it was the happiest period in Rafael's long life. They travelled America, these two outsiders, robbing just about every bank or stagecoach they came across, while bickering over politics and

the nature of God like two beautiful knight-errants on an end-
less quest to destroy the fabric of the American illusion, while
seducing her wives and emptying her purses.

And then the men reached Port Kydd.

"A dull Sodom," Rafael said.

"But one of rich purses," Jude said.

They made money, that was true. But there were problems.
Jude fell in love, with another. The Plain Barmaid, Rafael called
her. A simple plebeian unworthy of the brilliant Jude Kelly.

Though she had her charms. A fine cook. A fair conversa-
tionalist. A willingness to cut Jude down with her tongue when
he spoke too long of his ridiculous anarchist ideals. Yes, Rafael
understood the appeal of the Plain Barmaid, though he felt an
unending loneliness during the times Jude was not by his side.

But now they had a job to do. Smythe. The robbery went
down on November 1st. All Saints' Day.

The men guarding Smythe's warehouse were drunk. The
bounty easy for two experienced thieves.

"Simple," Jude said.

"Too simple," Rafael said.

Though Rafael worried about the ease of their larceny, he
couldn't turn down a celebration. For the next week, they lived
on fine dinners and many bottles from the Plain Barmaid's tavern. Rafael toasted to the coming child, promising he would be
the babe's eternal protector, the godfather he had never had.

"To the future," Jude toasted.

"And the child," the Plain Barmaid said.

"And revenge," Rafael said.

But they should have run, Rafael knew. Baby or not. They
should have known a man like Smythe wouldn't tolerate theft.
Rich men leave no grudge unfulfilled.

On the Feast of St. Nicholas, the last day of Rafael's first
life, when even amidst the sorrow of exile, there remained an

overwhelming joy in his heart and a lack of seriousness in his stance, Rafael stood on a rocky shore overlooking the Crabbe Sound, urinating, when a great cacophony emerged from the west and overtook the heavens. He turned, dumbfounded, believing that the hand of God sought to wash away all of humanity. Rafael buttoned his trousers, then fell to his knees.

There was nothing left to do but ready himself for the afterlife by recounting his sins. Yet where to begin for a professional thief and coveter of neighbors' wives?

Could he, perhaps, just ask the Lord for absolution, en masse? Or must he list every single sin? Was there time? And if he succeeded, would he be able to face his father in heaven without utter shame?

He bowed his head and began, "*Padre, yo renuncio a Satanás y todas sus obras, y yo te doy mi vida.*"

"Get up you loon," Jude said.

He dragged Rafael *toward* the end times. It was madness. But then Jude pointed behind them to three men in dark suits, holding rifles.

"Pinkertons," Jude said, pulling Rafael into a mud-slick street near the Plain Barmaid's tavern.

"I shall not run like a coward," Rafael said, before turning to the three ruffians just as they were on him. *Collette* made quick work of the first two, but the third fought without honor, tackling Rafael, punching him with the butt of his rifle. And just as Rafael believed he was to meet St. Peter, the man's head fell away, blood and brain falling onto Rafael's fine vest. He had been shot, Rafael figured, by Jude.

On his feet, he looked around for Jude before spotting a blanch of white hair in the mud while a Lilliputian dressed as a priest stood over him, alongside another man, this one with a fine suit and mutton chops. The men fired into Jude again and again.

Chapter Thirty-Nine

Rafael charged but stopped short.

Jude was dead, he knew.

He fell into the mud, wept.

There, he saw, out of the corner of his eye, a sight that stopped his prayers and altered his belief in a just God.

A young Black child, also dead in the street.

"Get the Negro."

It took a moment for Rafael to realize they meant him. Although he was a *Californio*, he knew that simple beasts of the Bonny saw all bronzed men as a danger.

The mob charged.

Rafael fled until he jumped into the Sound, where he hid behind a boulder for the longest three hours of his life. At times, he considered revealing himself, so death could take him quickly. But then he remembered the Plain Barmaid and Jude's child. If he were to offer himself to the mob, Rafael knew Jude would forever hate him in the afterlife.

So, when night fell, Rafael returned to the tavern and offered his eternal loyalty.

"For Jude."

CHAPTER FORTY

<u>October 29, 1929—Port Kydd, USA</u>

The morning after Hess died, Joshua leaned against the front door watching Lily's taxi pull away. She was going to her parents' house where she'd stay for the foreseeable future, including, Joshua figured, the days and weeks after the birth of their child. This wasn't his idea. In those hours after she shot Hess, when he and Rafael rolled Hess' body into a rug and then dumped him, she'd gone upstairs to pack a suitcase. There'd been no crying, no yelling. She'd packed in a mechanical manner like she had no power over the decision. He'd helped her down to the door and waited silently alongside her before the cab pulled up. She got in, looked at the driver, and Joshua shut the door. Her father would come around if she needed anything else. If people had noticed the split in the Riverses' marriage, if they'd seen the deadness in her eyes and the red in his, no one said anything. The whole neighborhood walked past Joshua as if he were a stranger. The shunning wouldn't stop, even as his life burned up on their front stoop.

He went downstairs, stepping over the well-mopped floor, and drained two whiskeys. He poured a third and went around the bar, singing to himself, filling the silence of the room with his voice, with the stomp of his boots, circling the long table, trying his best not to look at it. He tapped a couple of keys on the piano, startling Orla awake, and then stopped at the bookshelf and looked at the titles. He'd never actually picked up any of the books there, never read a single word from them. Most were old romances from the 1840s and 50s, books shelved by Nellie's mother. Others had been brought in over the years, including a hardback of *Don Quixote*, along with Jude Kelly's copy of *Common Sense*. Joshua drank a fourth whiskey and fell asleep against the piano.

He woke feeling no time had passed, like he'd been put under with chloroform. Orla sat on the stairs barking at the door. No one was knocking but he felt a presence in the bar, like someone had snuck in and was watching him. But what would he do?

Nothing.

He'd do nothing. He'd sit there and take it and do nothing. That's who he'd become.

"What is it, old girl?"

Orla came over and nuzzled his leg so he got her leash and then took his gun, reloaded it, and headed out for a walk.

It was three in the afternoon by then. There was a tremor in his hand and he couldn't get used to the sunlight on that brilliant day, a day without humidity, a day that was neither hot nor cool. The air felt like that beach in California but he wouldn't lose himself in that dream because he was still in the Bonny and no one would look at him and he had no plans for avoiding jail or getting his wife to come home and even if she did come home—because of money, because divorce was difficult—she would always look at him and remember the man who'd almost raped him, the man she *had to kill* to save her husband. He walked north as the signs switched from English to Yiddish.

The smell of pastrami cooking came out of delis, while leaves drizzled to the sidewalk in a way that reminded him of some of his grandmother's paintings. If he got the chance, he thought, he'd burn every last canvas.

Near Lafitte Square, he bought a tube of salami for Orla and then sat on a bench in a small park dedicated to the fallen soldiers of the Great War. They'd planned on building a statue of a doughboy but no one ever got around to it. Instead, there was a poorly kept lawn and a few benches looking out at a quiet street. He smoked another cigarette while hand-feeding Orla. A row of brick apartments, built just after the War, framed the park. At the second-floor window of a corner apartment, a woman with wild gray hair talked beside the window, or, knowing her as he did, yelled at someone in the next room. He couldn't hear her voice but he imagined the gist of it—*Did I not tell you he was no good? On your wedding day, remember, I promised he would be the one to break your heart.* It wasn't long before Lily emerged into view.

After she'd shot Hess, after she kept pulling the trigger long after the last bullet, Rafael took the gun and held her to his chest, and then motioned for Joshua to find his clothes. He put them on, faced away from his wife, looking all the while at the old revolutionary, the old soldier with his stiff posture and cold lips. Joshua always figured he was the unknown "father" of the Swill, a man, like all the men of the Swill, who'd dropped his seed and abandoned the woman to the elements. In the right light, there was a vague resemblance between him and Joshua. The nose was a bit Roman, the eyes narrow and blue. He looked like he was good at cards and ran away when women cried.

"Fucking Olive," he said. "Why did she do this to me?"

Orla waited for another piece of salami.

"Is this the first sign of insanity?" Joshua said. "Expecting a dog to answer."

Chapter Forty

He walked Orla toward the Crabbe.

On his way a paperboy yelped about broke stockmen and suicides and shut factories. The President said the crisis would pass, that it was a minor hiccup on our path toward continued prosperity. Joshua bought a paper and leaned against a phone booth and read through a story on Smythe Holdings' falling stock, on Jasper laying off hundreds of workers at his iron-works, at his opponent blaming the crash on Jasper himself.

He tossed the paper and then went down to the shore and out to the edge of an old, sagging pier to look at the dark water. A coal barge motored north toward the Canal. Trains rumbled behind him. He looked for the boat to Flywell but didn't see it.

"You thinking of jumping, Mister?"

Orla growled and Joshua whipped around and found a girl, twenty at most, dressed like she'd just gotten off a cabaret stage. Her eyes were bagged and her hair had grass trapped just above her ear. She'd probably slept in a park that night and hadn't bothered with a mirror afterward.

"You hear me, Mister? You don't need to jump, not with the mutt, at least. Your troubles ain't his fault."

He lit a cigarette. She asked for one and he ignored her.

"You're not much of a talker, are you?" she said.

He leaned against the railing while the wind blew smoke into his eyes.

"It's real pretty out here, real pretty," she said. "Where I'm from, out west, you've got none of this water. Sometimes you go weeks without seeing enough rain to fill a bucket. Texas is where I'm from. El Paso. Yep, got to be sixteen and got myself on a train and I've been moving ever since. You probably don't know what that's like. You look like you're from these parts. The way your shoulders slump, says it all to me. That's okay. This is a fine place to be from, a fine place to stay."

Joshua grunted.

Chapter Forty

"Times are hard though. People keep saying that this week. Last week they said times were good, that these were the good old days and I guess they were because the good old days are gone and now everyone is looking for work. I was working at this factory last week, sewing buttons on sweaters. All day long, I just sewed buttons. Not like they used to, right, not with a needle and thread but they got this machine that makes it quicker, so you can sew three buttons a minute but now that's gone. It was hard work on my hands. See, look at my hands. Look."

She was right. Her hands were calloused.

"What's going on in that mind of yours?" she asked. "We don't know each other. Makes me better than a preacher. I'm not going to judge you. I just want to hear someone's voice that isn't mine."

He stepped back, looked her over.

"You don't want to hear it," he said.

"Sure I do. I like a good story. Come on. Give me a try."

"You want to hear it? Fine. There's a man in Collier Park I'm supposed to kill but I can't do it. I'm supposed to, you know? I'm supposed to because that's what people expect me to do. To be a man who kills another man. That's how this story is supposed to go but I can't do it. I'm supposed to be a tough guy like all the guys I grew up with but I ain't that anymore. It's just gone. Knew a guy back in the War, who all of a sudden stopped drinking coffee. Just said his body had told him he'd had his last cup. And we were tired. Up all night marching, on sentry, but he was just done with coffee. That's how I feel. I'm done being tough, just want to be left alone but no one will let me. Yeah, I brought some of it on myself. Did something stupid for money but I can't keep acting like I'm the kind of guy I'm supposed to be. I just want to sit at the ocean and raise my kid."

Chapter Forty

As he spoke this, she backed away, scared. "Mister, I just wanted to hear something sweet and you got to go get all truthful on me. There isn't no call for that."

He pulled out his gun, turned and fired off all six rounds toward Flywell. When he looked back, she was running down the dock, a straw of a girl, far from home. At the edge of the pier, she stopped and screamed. It was windy, so he wasn't sure he heard it right, but he thought she said, "You're a real son of a bitch."

He turned back toward the water and studied the gun. It had been issued to him on November 18th, 1917. There'd been a sheen about it then. So much possibility. Now it was dulled, tarnished. He held it out over the water, and then let it fall.

CHAPTER FORTY-ONE

He left Orla at home and then spent the rest of the evening with a bottle. He searched Pinebox Square for Olive, not knowing what he'd say if he found her. Meanwhile, cops and private detectives patrolled the street corners and searched the alleyways, knocking around young girls they thought perverted, asking after Olive. Some of these hired thugs saw him, nodded his way, realized who he was, and knew not to bother asking after his sister. A brother wouldn't talk. Others looked right through him like he was just another lowlife looking for a fix. He couldn't blame them. He imagined he appeared as rough as he had in France, at the end. Rougher, he thought. He'd been ten years younger then.

That old image of himself back in 1918 got him thinking and thinking—he'd discovered—got him into trouble, so he walked around some more, stumbling into garbage cans, into passing strangers, until, whether by luck or fate, he found himself in front of the Port Kydd Veterans Lodge. Under the archway, he drank the last of his bottle and then aimed it at a passing taxi but on the throw it slipped from his hand, bouncing limply to the curb.

Chapter Forty-One

"Fucking fucks."

He pushed into the lodge's smoky light. A pair of old timers, Spanish war vets, bent over the bar playing chess, while a few younger men, guys from *his war*, played cards at a back table. A couple of American flags hung from the wall, one with 36 stars and the other with 48. In the middle of the hall sat a table full of cookies, cakes, and a casserole. A boxing match played softly on the radio.

"Hey buddy, you all right?"

"What?"

The bartender waved at him. He was a young guy with an anchor tattoo on his bicep. A pin on his lapel said he'd served on the *Missouri*.

"You all right, buddy?"

"What?"

"You need some help?"

"Whiskey."

Joshua reached for a stool, balancing, before sliding onto it, holding tight to the bar, which shimmered in reds and greens like a Christmas tree. Next to him, the old men paused their chess, while the bartender filled a glass with ice and then wavered over the bottle.

"We've got some coffee," the bartender said. "It's not good but it's strong."

"You new around here?" said the old man playing white on the chessboard. "Port Kydd is a lovely town, despite its reputation. A really friendly people. Good-hearted. The winters are difficult but the spring is worth the hard months. Generous folks, I've found. Good old-fashioned values."

Joshua ran his fingers over the bar's smoothed-over lacquer. No scars from wear and tear. Like the rest of the building, it had been built after the last war, during flush times.

"Whiskey."

Chapter Forty-One

"How about some coffee. Looks like it would be good for you."

Two of the younger men came up beside and put their mugs on the bar. They wore hats from the 29th. Joshua had enlisted in Texas, fighting out of the 34th but had run into their unit near Puvenville, before the Battle of Château-Thierry, his first fight of the War. The bartender came over with some coffee, while the old man playing black offered a plate of casserole and a cookie.

"Here," he said. "Eat a little."

"Eat?" Joshua asked.

"Where you from?" asked one of the younger men.

"Where did you serve?" said the old man.

Joshua hesitated, trying to understand the question.

"Where did I serve?" he finally said. "Well—"

CHAPTER FORTY-TWO

…A green ceiling and a soft mattress. Typewriters. An intermittent squawk in his head. Blood in his mouth. His gut pulsated, bruised….

…"Wake up, ya fuckin' cocksucker. Wake up before aye put ya on the boat to Flywell…"

…a nightstick slapping steel. Crying. Bleach and the wringing of a mop….

…And when he finally awoke, he rolled onto his side, his wrists bruised, and beyond him lay prison bars and a harsh, blinking light on the free side.

"Ugh, goddammit."

He tried to go back to sleep, but when he couldn't, he found Detective Duffy on the other side of the iron bars, sitting beside an interrogation lamp, reading a book. Joshua's eyes hurt too much to make out the title.

"Good evening," Duffy said.

Joshua sat upright, gut drumming. He grabbed it and groaned.

"Yeah, the bartender said he gave you a good shot to put you down. The old man with the chessboard gave you the headache."

Chapter Forty-Two

He wiped his mouth and came away with bloody fingers. "Ah, shit."

"About says it, Shakespeare. You remember your trip to the vets' hall?"

"No. Well. I don't know. Remember going there, I think. Where am I?"

"Do you remember them kicking the hell out of you for being an asshole?"

Joshua didn't.

"Better that way," Duffy said. "A wise man once said that if you're going to take on six guys, make sure they're monks."

"You that goddamn wise man?"

"See they didn't kick the asshole out of you."

"What did I say?"

"To the vets?" Duffy put down his book and passed Joshua a cigarette. "Well, from the police report, it seems you gave a grand talk about the pointlessness of war, the betrayal of American values led by the late President Wilson, and the stupidity of man before you talked about all the people you killed and how you did it, going into great detail about the love you had for a knife named Mrs. O'Toole and about the half-dozen men you gutted with her and how if you had a son you'd sooner chain him to a radiator than let him fight for Uncle Sam. They took exception to that. Should I go on?"

"No."

Duffy unlocked the cell to sit on the cot beside Joshua. There were three other cells on the block, each empty, the beds made with military precision and the toilets shined. It was a very nice jail.

"This isn't Flywell," Joshua said.

"No, it's the drunk-tank in Uptown. A beautiful new cop shop with only the finest blackjacks money can buy. Brought you up here this morning from the rat cage they stuck you down in Pinebox Square."

"Yesterday?"

"Yes, Rip Van Winkle. You've been out nearly twenty hours. The old man with the chessboard should look into playing some ball. He did a number on your eye worse than the one I gave you on the chin."

He then remembered insulting everyone in the vets' lodge—calling the lot of them cowards—right before a 70-year-old man who'd fought beside Teddy Roosevelt dropped him with a granite chessboard. His face fell into his hands and he groaned, from regret, from the throbbing in his eye.

"Look, I like you, Rivers. I really do. I think deep down you're a decent enough man, just prone to making the occasional dumb decision. I feel bad about that knock I gave you and I feel bad about my part in this mess. You know I did join the police out of a sense of duty. Sure wasn't the money. Even if you're skimming a bit, which I ain't, not really, not much, not enough to get me better shoes and a nicer wife. At first, you think you're doing good work, protecting the innocent, putting the not-so-innocent in a place where they can't do any harm but then you find that you're always showing up on somebody's worst day, the absolute worst day of someone's life and you haven't done anything to protect them. You're just cleaning up the mess. But you do what you can to give them comfort and maybe you're good at that, so they promote you and then you find out that your job isn't to protect the innocent or even comfort but to protect private property and those men aren't innocent at all. Justice, right?"

Joshua groaned.

"Well, here's the thing," Duffy said. "Found a body outside Smythe's building. Can't say for sure, given the state of the corpse's face, but it looks like it was his boy Hess. You wouldn't know anything about that, would you?"

"No." Joshua ran his finger through his mouth. He was missing a couple of teeth. "Duffy, how bad is it? Just level with me."

"Remember what I said would happen if we couldn't find your sister, well, we're there now."

"How long?"

"What?"

"You know what I'm asking."

"Armed robbery and assaulting a cop gets you ten to fifteen, but my guess is a year or two, tops. You've got the wife and the baby and people tend to not hate you right off, though it's tougher once they get to know you."

"1931, 32."

"That's the math. Two years is still short time. Your sister does twenty given how she's going to be painted in a deviant light. Look, your wife and Castillo can hold down the bar while you're gone. Some other folks in the Bonny might pick up some of the slack. Rivers, you okay? Rivers?" Duffy began to pace. "I know it's hard. I understand but in the course of a man's long life, a year or two is something you can forget."

The rats at Flywell had run over his ankles all night long. The Italian with the baseball had begged for his life as the prison guard strangled him.

"Could you survive a year or two?"

Duffy was about to answer when the door to the cellblock opened and in stepped Jasper Smythe, hair mussed along his sideburns, and a face that looked almost as rough as Joshua's. If he'd never met Jasper, Joshua would swear the man had also been crying.

"Take it he's under arrest," Joshua said.

Duffy smoothed out his suit and walked out of the jail cell to meet Jasper.

"Sir, are you sure you want to be in a place like this? The papers get ahold—"

"Are there any newspapermen out there, Detective?" Jasper asked. "No, there aren't, so I suspect we'll be just fine under the circumstances."

"Yes, sir."

Joshua held out his cigarette, looking at the fire, at the way the smoke curled into the air. He didn't remember any cigarettes on Flywell. The guards had stolen them all.

"Do you sit on his lap and let him pet you?" Joshua said to Duffy.

Duffy stepped into the cell, drew back his hand, and swung. Joshua let the cigarette go on his way to the floor. It had rolled under his cot and he reached out, grabbing it with the tips of his fingers, before climbing to his knees.

"Ah, did you have to hit the good eye?"

"Get up, Rivers," Duffy said, pulling him up to the cot. "You'd do better to listen than talk."

"Justice, right?" Joshua said.

Duffy stepped out of the cell and Jasper came in. The rich man loomed over Joshua, blocking the light, death in a wrinkled suit. Jasper reached down, his hand taking hold of Joshua's jaw, lifting it.

"I wouldn't do that, sir," Duffy said.

"Why, detective? Is this man really capable of killing me before you could step in?"

"Yes," Duffy said. "He most certainly is."

Jasper let go, stepped back, and crossed his arms.

"Talk," Jasper said.

"I think," Joshua said, his head clouding, his eyes drifting to the floor.

"What?" Jasper asked.

"I'm a little dizzy," Joshua said. "What did you say?"

Chapter Forty-Two

"Talk."

"Okay, okay. I think, I think I'm going to vote for the other guy."

Jasper turned to Duffy.

"Probably just too many knocks on the head," Duffy said. "You have to be more specific, sir."

"Sir, ha," Joshua said. "What do you want to talk about, Smythe?"

"Mr. Hess, for one," Jasper said. "And then the paintings."

"You hire soldiers, they sometimes die," Joshua said.

"A confession," Jasper said.

"Seems more like a hastily constructed aphorism," Duffy said. "Rivers did you kill Hess?"

"No."

"Where is your sister?" Jasper said.

"I don't care."

Duffy leaned toward Jasper and whispered.

"Kindness?" Jasper said. "Well, looking at him, I guess violence has proved futile. Fine but keep your gun out."

Duffy took out his gun.

Jasper stepped toward Joshua, took out a handkerchief, and then as Joshua reached for it, Jasper wiped down the empty part of the cot, and sat.

"Mr. Rivers. This is a moment for brutal honesty."

Joshua looked at his bare feet. "Someone stole my shoes. My damn shoes."

"Your coat too," Duffy said. "They fleeced you good."

"Honesty," Jasper began, as if he'd rehearsed this speech. "For a man in my position is often a liability. No one values honesty. They value the illusion of forthrightness. Honesty brings shame. My mother knew this."

"Your mother?"

214

"Yes. She kept secrets. Her love of laudanum. An affair with an associate of my father's. Her enjoyment of your grandmother's company."

He paused, wiping his eyes. It was all a performance, Joshua saw. There was nothing honest happening in this jail cell.

"Your grandmother provided my mother with a much-needed respite from the grueling conformity of her life. For that, I am indebted to your family."

"And now comes the stick," Joshua said.

"I don't want to send you to prison," Jasper said. "But your sister or you must be arrested for the robbery. Suspicion must not cloud these last two weeks of my campaign."

"Why can't your kind just let us be."

"My kind, Mr. Rivers, built this town. My kind built that grand library and the railway station and the waterworks and the very streets themselves. Without my kind, your kind would still live in mud huts."

Joshua laid his head in his hands, let the dizziness run its course.

"If we're not careful," Joshua said, "this is going to end bad for all of us because we're all too stupid to walk away. All of this over some dead relatives and old canvases. It's like the War. There isn't no real reason to it except we're trying to make meaning out of nothing. All those dead Negroes and we're still trying to make ourselves look good."

"Are you a nihilist now, Mr. Rivers?"

"I don't know what the hell I am."

Jasper stepped out of the cell and told Duffy to talk some sense into him before disappearing down the hall.

"Sir? Sir? How do his boots taste?"

"We all got mouths to feed Rivers. You know how this town works. Look, you've got a choice. Give us Olive or do time. That's coming from the Chief."

Chapter Forty-Two

"I can't find her."

"Look, you've got 'till five tomorrow, then we're coming for you. It's not enough time to run. You know we'll have you before you hit the Mississippi. So you'd better find her, for your sake."

"You're an asshole Duffy. Even for a cop, you're one of the world's great assholes."

CHAPTER FORTY-THREE

Outside, the moon rose over the Sound just as the sun sent its last sparks out west, and Joshua Rivers, ex-soldier and barman, had no shoes and no coat and was thirty blocks from home. He hadn't a dollar for a cab or a nickel for a phone and even if he had, there was no one who would take his call. The wind slapped cold from the north and he crossed his arms just in time to feel the pain in his ribs. If he could have seen well enough out of his two bruised, blackened eyes, he'd have noticed women dragging their children across the street and petty thieves giving sympathetic nods.

This, he knew, could be his last night of freedom for a long time.

Still, he walked home.

PART SIX: HALLOWS BY THE ROADSIDE

CHAPTER FORTY-FOUR

December 21st, 1928

A man she'd worked with before told Olive to go the library. "Go to the atrium," he said. "Trust me."

"Ha," she said.

But she went anyways because she was broke and because she was bored. On a snowy December morning, she arrived at the library dressed in black, with a funeral veil and a handkerchief to dab her eyes. Walk with a mourning pose. Never case a joint without a costume. Don't want some guard with a rich memory fingering you to the cops.

In the atrium, under the blue light, she saw four paintings "from the Smythe Collection" and knew it was the view from her grandmother's bedroom window. She'd known her grandmother was a painter. Had heard stories from Miss Amand and others from the old generation. But she could never imagine her grandmother as good enough for some place as posh as the library. Girls from the Bonny *forged* paintings. They didn't create them from scratch.

She forgot her costume for a second. "Holy hell," she said, as others passed by.

Chapter Forty-Four

Each painting named on a nearby plate.

Downtown in summer.

All Saints Riot.

Aristocrat, nude.

The Passenger Pigeons.

The first two didn't interest her; she'd seen the Bonny both in summer and in chaos. The third, the nude, she later discovered was of Mary Smythe, herself. A real looker. Wife to the man who'd killed Jude Kelly.

The last painting got stuck in her head like a nursery rhyme. Delighting her at first. Torturing her thereafter. She knew the story.

The last arrival of the Passenger Pigeons.

The day of the Great Bonny Riot.

The reason Blacks avoided the Bonny.

There were songs.

"The Devil's from the Bonny."

"The Bloody Bonny Blues."

"A Body in the Bonny."

Lamentations for the dead. Curses toward the Bonny and her evil white men. Fair enough, Olive thought. We had it coming.

Seventeen dead, she knew. Seventeen dead men, women, and children, all Black, save one Canadian. Her grandfather. His killers were there. Billy-Bailey Vanderhock. Maynard Smythe.

Another victim, Rafael Castillo. Broken thereafter. Perpetual grief. Sacrificed his dreams to care for Jude's child. A blood oath, he once told Olive. No matter how much he wanted to leave, he could never abandon Jude's family.

Her grandmother never talked about that day. Refused to have it spoken in her presence. Rafael was the same. *No lo se.* Only Miss Amand spoke of it, called it the town's most shameful day, a black scar never to heal. But no one listened to her except Olive. The entire neighborhood attempted to forget. Not from pain or guilt, she thought. But pride. They didn't want to think they were the kind of people to do that. They were.

So Olive had sought out the truth, from a young age. It was because she knew she was different, knew the nuns thought her evil. Would the neighborhood do the same to her? That was her fear. She loved it and hated it. Saw the good and the evil. The blessings and sins. One moment a hand of grace fell upon your shoulder and a moment later that hand pulled a switchblade. Or, even worse, took away your voice.

How to reconcile the love of the Bonny and the hate? That was her question from an early age, from the moment she understood the truth about herself and knew the truth would disappear her.

This picture was her grandmother's reconciliation of that duality. Forget it. Never speak of it. No more questions.

Nellie Rivers had stopped time the moment before her lover was gunned down by Billy-Bailey Vanderhock's lousy aim and Maynard Smythe's steady hand. That must have been her motive, Olive thought. To forget.

But still this painting was a lie. One first forged by her grandmother's hand and then propagated by Smythe's son. For money. It was always about money in Port Kydd. There were profits in forgetting.

So what was a girl to do?

CHAPTER FORTY-FIVE

<u>October 29, 1929—Port Kydd, USA</u>

When he reached the Swill, the door was unlocked and the lights were on. He knew it wasn't Lily or Rafael. And his sister wasn't foolish enough to come back here. So it had to be some-one else and everyone else wanted him dead or broken. Keep walking, he thought, but his feet bled from broken glass and his teeth chattered from the cold and he was too tired to turn around and too beaten up to make a fist, so he went down the stairs ready to take what was given.

It wasn't who he expected.

Raab, the librarian, stood shirtless, arms raised like a stat-ue. Orla sat at his feet, submissive. Raab slowly brought his arms into a boxer's stance, except his palms were out and his gaze had an angelic appearance as though he was completely at peace. He held his pose, eyes fixed at the bar mirror, and then said, "You are perhaps wondering what I am doing?"

"A bit," Joshua said.

"Tai chi, an ancient Chinese art of self-defense."

"Okay."

"You have a very good dog. What is her breed?"

Chapter Forty-Five

"Irish pub terrier. Used to taste the food for the ancient kings of Ireland."

"You jest but she is lovely and you do not deserve her."

Orla looked done with Joshua. He'd been in lockup for two days and hadn't been home to feed her.

"Thanks for taking care of her."

"Consider it recompense for the generosity you showed by not beating me in the library this past spring."

"I don't know what you're talking about."

"Of course you do. Your sister said it was you."

"Of course she did."

Raab dropped his pose, picked up a glass of water, and took a long look at Joshua. "My god, man, what have they done to you?"

Raab picked off some ice from a block and brought it to Joshua in a towel and Joshua put the ice in a glass and poured gin on top of it.

"It was for your eye," Raab said.

"This works quicker." He took a drink and poured a second. "So, let me guess. You're Olive's fence and probably the go-between with Jasper."

Raab nodded.

"And she backstabbed you and the people you sold the paintings to are angry because you sold them fakes."

Raab nodded.

"And it won't take long for Jasper to think you double-crossed him."

Raab pointed at a large suitcase next to the piano and a blanket on the floor beside it.

"You could have used one of the beds upstairs."

"That seems rather rude."

Joshua poured one for Raab. "So how'd you get mixed up with Olive?"

"It's a long story."

"Is it?"

"No."

A few years back, he'd hired Olive to steal a rare book from the library—myths written in Old Norse—and she'd done such a stellar job that he went back to her several times over the years. She'd robbed a dodo from the Port Kydd Natural History Museum, a Botticelli from the Collier Park Art Gallery, and even took a 17th century Dutch Bible from Vanderhock's church. So when Smythe expressed a desire to get rid of the paintings—first by selling them to rich men not concerned with legality and second for the insurance money—Raab had thought of her. But she'd double-crossed him.

Joshua sat at the bar and put the glass to his eye. "My sister is some piece of work, isn't she? She must have got it from her father, whoever the hell he was. You here to take a shot at her? I won't blame you."

"Revenge is the poor man's choice. No, Mr. Rivers, I am running."

"So why aren't you gone then?"

"Benevolence and empathy, Mr. Rivers. Benevolence and empathy. Because you chose not to hurt me, I choose to repay the kindness, a second time."

"A second time?"

"The warden of Flywell Island is an old school chum of mine. I made a call, brought some cash, and he let you free."

"Thank you. You're not bad for a librarian."

"Well, it is not just for you. I must admit that after this whole ordeal, I don't particularly like Smythe."

"Sounds more like spite," Joshua said.

"Call it civic duty," Raab said. "The hubris of the man already dwarfs his talent. He'll believe himself the next coming of Augustus, while we suffer under his Nero-like failures."

He handed Joshua a large envelope. Inside there was an odd type of photograph, the kind Vanderhock had done on his thumb.

"You might find this helpful. It's the X-ray of the first painting we found," Raab said. "Look closely."

Joshua couldn't see anything at first, just a mess of white lines crisscrossing as if a child drew them. Then slowly, as his eyes oriented, he began to make out the sweeping image of *The Passenger Pigeons* and then, as if he'd changed the lens on his irises, he saw that beneath it another painting, this one a woman on a shore, wearing a lush gown, one out of style by about a century.

"At first, I couldn't make heads nor tails of it," Raab said, "but then I awoke in the middle of the night with great clarity. This portrait was commissioned by Maynard Smythe for his wife in 1870."

"Mary Smythe?" Joshua asked.

"Yes, Jasper's mother. Well, this portrait was in storage in the library the last time I checked. Your sister must have stolen it. If you look at the X-rays of the others, you'll find other portraits of Mary, all completed around this time. Horribly sentimental portraits, not worth a cent. Your sister is trying to torture Jasper. She painted over his old family portraits knowing full well that someone would take an X-ray of them. I told Jasper's insurance company my findings yesterday morning. None of the paintings are legitimate. All of the stolen paintings remain in the wind. They don't know what to think, but they feel that Smythe is connected, that he has sought to defraud the insurance company somehow by selling the originals."

"Why would he sell the originals and then have forgeries made up?" Joshua said. "The money is in those paintings never showing up again."

"It's a good point, Mr. Rivers," Raab said. "I asked the insurance investigator just that and do you know what he said. He said, 'Sir, I have met Mr. Smythe and if I was a thief in his employ, I'd betray him as soon as the money allowed.'"

"Smart man," Joshua said. "But also means you're running."

"Exactly. You might consider doing the same."

"It's too late for that," Joshua said.

"Perhaps, Mr. Rivers. But a wise man once said 'forewarned, forearmed'; to be prepared is half the victory."

Joshua raised his hand to his chin. "I've had it up to here with wise men. When are you leaving town?"

"Tomorrow evening," Raab said. "There is a man who uses the old smuggler tunnels as—"

"Roche."

"Yes."

"You know he might double-cross you as well."

"Perhaps," Raab said, pulling out a .36 revolver. "But that is why the God above gave us firearms. For five hundred dollars, Roche'd give you berth on the boat as well."

"I'll think about it but, well, since this might be my last night of freedom, I'm going to have another drink. Will you join me for another?"

"A wise man once said—"

"Drink."

CHAPTER FORTY-SIX

In the morning, Joshua awoke against the piano to the sound of pounding on the front door. He hadn't remembered going to sleep and figured he'd drunk himself into darkness but when he felt for his head, expecting the hangover, it wasn't there. On the floor, beside the piano, lay Raab. He was in his underwear, Orla asleep by his head. The librarian, Joshua remembered, convinced him to give up the bottle for a night, and instead made him talk sober. It had been a dark conversation about the War, about his feelings toward community, courage, and violence—a conflict he was still trying to work out in his head—and then the evening took a strange turn, one involving odd Chinese poses, along with deep breathing exercises done while sitting Indian style. They had ended the night singing Irish folk tunes.

But now it was morning and the knocks kept coming so he looked in the bar mirror, his eyes blackened, but his hair was starting to grow back. He went through the junk box, found his grandmother's old gun, one that would probably blow his hand off if he tried to fire it, and then went upstairs, expecting a delivery or the cops but who he saw instead was Neal Stephens holding two cups of coffee.

"Good morning," Neal said, handing one over to Joshua, while ignoring the gun. "You know when you ask for a regular coffee in this town, they give you three creams, two sugars, and a shot of bourbon?"

"Yeah, it's in the town charter."

"Magnificent. Just magnificent."

This was a guy who hadn't been sober since he was in short pants but still looked like he could give Douglas Fairbanks a run for most handsome. He pushed past Joshua to head down the stairs. No invitation.

"Lily's not here," Joshua said, following him.

"I know. She asked me to come over and pick up some of her things."

"Thought she'd send her father."

"I met the old man yesterday. Pretty sure you prefer me."

Neal stopped on the landing, looked at Raab and Orla, and then shrugged on his way to a stool. Joshua joined him and they sat for a while sipping their coffee. Neal offered Joshua a cigarette and he took it.

"Thanks, I ran out," Joshua said.

Neal took three more and passed them down the bar and Joshua put them in his shirt pocket. "You'd make an excellent executioner," Joshua said. "Guess that's your job today."

"Not sure it's that bad. She didn't say anything mean about you, if that's what you're wondering. Just said it was best to be with her folks with things how they are, the baby and, well, you being in the muck with just about everyone."

Neal took a drink. "It's good coffee. Not the best I've ever had, but good. Best coffee I had, oddly enough, was in San Francisco. The Yerba Buena Café on the wharf. The woman making it, a cute little number, came from Vienna. Still remember the taste of it. Made all the diner coffee I've drunk taste like cheap swill, pun intended, of course."

Chapter Forty-Six

"Yep."

"Now I've had espresso in Paris and Rome, even had a cup of coffee in Brazil right on a coffee plantation but nothing beat this cup in San Francisco."

"What were you doing in Brazil?"

"Looking for my father." Neal mashed out his cigarette, shook his head. "No, that's a lie. It just seemed, at the time, like a good place to go, to—"

"Hide?"

"In a manner of speaking, yes. You've been around. Where would you get your last cup of coffee?"

"The Yerba Buena Café."

"No kidding?"

"And her name was Pia."

"Pia," Neal said. "Ha, never asked."

"Was good coffee," Joshua said. He held up his cup. "This isn't bad though."

"The bourbon rounds it out."

"How is Lily otherwise?"

"A bit shellshocked, if you don't mind the phrase."

"Accurate enough."

"She told me what happened. Or enough. Sorry. She stares out the window a lot, holding her stomach. Doesn't talk much except to yell at her mother to leave her alone. Isn't sleeping."

"I want her to come home."

Neal went over to Raab, crouched, and then put two fingers to the man's jugular. Orla growled. "That a good idea?" Neal said. "You're answering the door with a gun and that baby is going to be coming any day now."

Joshua went around the bar and poured himself a glass of water.

"Fair enough. Well, come on up so you can grab what you need."

CHAPTER FORTY-SEVEN

Joshua went looking for Olive but had no idea what he'd do when he found her. If he turned her in, the cops would kill her. If he didn't give her up, the cops would kill him or lock him up on Flywell. If he ran, he'd be abandoning his wife and child and would probably get caught anyways. So he looked for Olive but it was a passive sort-of search. He hoped the journey itself would decide the ending. He started at the Cooke Village apartment where she'd been shot, finding a few cops mulling around a white chalk outline in the alleyway. He checked the bars in Pinebox Square again. He returned to the railroad apartment where she painted the forgeries. He didn't know where else his sister frequented, so he wandered the streets for a while, looking for a woman with blonde hair. Eventually, he reached uptown, amidst the grid of high rises and fine suits and expensive hats and then stopped in front of the Port Kydd Central Railway Station, which, in Joshua's mind, was the most beautiful building on the Island.

It had been built in 1880 out of a mountain of granite. Taking up five square blocks, the station had a neoclassical look, with grand cornices and columns supporting the towering archway.

Chapter Forty-Seven

It even had windows framed with statues of Roman goddesses. It made you feel like you lived in a better, more civilized place. He wondered if that was Maynard Smythe's idea, because, like the library, the station had been funded out of his pocket, a way for the rich to reach immortality. Outside, Joshua bought a hot dog and then joined the wave pushing inside and found a seat in the central concourse and ate amongst a crowd of lovers kissing goodbye and children greeting long away fathers. Cops searched for his sister, he figured, but perhaps were also tasked with keeping an eye out for him as well. The display board updated departure times for points west. There was a train leaving for California at 8pm. On the arched ceiling, there was a mural of Port Kydd reminiscent of the old-style maps explorers used back in the times of Magellan. Even from one hundred feet below, Joshua could make out where the Bonny was and even approximately where the Swill stood. But it wasn't the whole of the Island up there. The city had been filling in the edges with gravel so that she could build more tenements and longer docks, so that she could make more money than geography and God had intended.

A cop ambled passed and Joshua lowered his eyes, just enough for the cop to give him a second look.

"Going anywhere ya fuck?" the cop said. "Ya thinkin' of getting on a train, think twice."

Joshua got up and on his way toward the door remembered the last time he'd been here, back when he had returned to take over the Swill, a 30-year-old man with twenty bucks in his pocket. He'd seen the world and knew, because of it, he was coming home a different man than the one who'd left on his 16th birthday. Five years later, he wasn't sure he was all that different. Even on the road or in the army, he'd lived at the edge of lawfulness, just getting by, always pulling some sort of scam, never fully committing to being where he was at that moment.

Chapter Forty-Seven

In the army, he ransacked Belgium homes for liquor and stole cigarettes from the commissary to sell out of the back of a jeep in town. Now, he was the type of guy who'd commit a robbery rather than accept that he was a husband and barman and almost a father. And look where it landed him? Back in a train station doing much the same as before. Nothing, he saw, had changed, except that when someone threw a punch, he didn't punch back. The violence inside of him was gone and now he was just a guy who took the easiest road available. And that, he knew, was the problem.

CHAPTER FORTY-EIGHT

When he got home, it was four o'clock, an hour before Roche was coming, an hour before Duffy said he'd show up, and there, at the bar, he found Raab with a drink, alongside Olive, who was washing glasses. She was dressed like a barmaid, with heavy makeup, a white apron, and her hair in a bun. She looked up from the dishes, saw him rooted to the landing, and said, "What are you drinking?"

"Water."

"You know we serve no such thing. Blasphemy. Old wenches are turning over in their graves. Now, will it be dark or light? You've got to choose."

"Light," he nodded. "But just half a pint."

"Ah. Trying to keep your girlish figure. I hear men go to fat when their wives are in a family way. I admire your resolve, big brother. I really do. Don't want her running around with the postman behind your back."

She smiled in an unfamiliar way. It seemed honest. Joshua went over and sat beside Raab. He listened for any noise upstairs, anything that would tip him off the cops had shown up early—as they were liable to do—but all he heard were the familiar intonations of a street gone sour, the screams and swears of an angry, spiteful people, the kind who turn their backs when the least bit of trouble comes down the road. The hell with all of them. He took a drink, felt a sickness rise. Tell her to run, he thought. Tell her. But he couldn't.

"I thought you two would be fighting to the death?" Joshua asked.

"What is betrayal in our line of work?" Raab asked. "We are better than our station, better than our reputation. We are civilized practitioners of—"

"I paid him off," Olive said.

"Yes she did."

"What are you doing here?" Joshua asked her.

"Feeling homesick."

"Olive?"

"Jesus, Joshua, you've been hollering my name all over town. Didn't you think I'd hear?"

"The cops—"

"Only know to look at the front door. They stare at the front door like all foolish men. Don't you think the women who built this bar had a second door in mind? A ladies' entrance."

There was the door by the old outhouses and the one to the caverns, but those seemed unlikely.

"So big brother, what did you want to talk about?" Olive said.

"What the hell do you think?"

"And with that," Raab said, picking up his suitcase, "I shall go wait for Mr. Roche. I hope, for both of your sakes, that you choose to join me."

After Raab went down to the cavern, Joshua peeked at the stairs that led up to the street, listening again, but heard nothing but the same. Run, Olive. Don't tell her. The voices in his head kept screaming. What did he want to talk about? All day he'd been thinking about this very moment and all day he had no idea what he would say to her. At this point, all he had left was the truth.

"Hess is dead."

"I heard." She smiled and stretched out her hand into a pistol. "Someone blew a hole in his head so big the cops—"

"Lily did it. Right over there." He pointed at the floor. "Lily shot him to save me."

Olive planted her eyes on her brother's own. "Huh, I didn't think she had it in her. Misread that girl."

"You did."

"Why didn't you just sink him in the Crabbe? Why prop him up like that for Smythe to see?"

"I wanted Jasper to know it. I wanted him to feel scared."

"Well, he's too rich to be scared, at least of you. You can't come straight at those types. No frontal assaults, no up and over into no-man's-land firing into the dark. You should know that, war hero. Putting a corpse on his front porch is like blowing the goddamn bugle."

Joshua lit a cigarette.

"Seems strange though," Olive said. "Can't see why Hess would try to kill you. He'd know I'd have to—"

"He didn't try to kill me. He didn't. He wasn't here to kill me."

He laid his head on the bar, felt an exhaustion that seemed unnatural, like the sleeping sickness taking hold.

"It's happened to me," Olive said. "Men have tried to, you know. I mean they've gotten close to it. Say all I need is a little roll to make me normal."

"It's not the same."

"The hell it isn't."

"It's more humiliating. It's more—"

"It's the same," Olive said. "Our pain is the same."

He felt an old fury rising but before he could let it loose, she held up her hand and said, "Hold onto that thought. I want to show you something first."

She kneeled behind the bar and he leaned over as she pulled up the panel, flipping it up and over before jumping in and landing on the wood below. At her height, she was shoulder-deep and if she crouched, just a bit, she could flip over the panel and hide just fine and no one, not unless he had a keen eye, would find her. But she wasn't hiding. Her hand ran along the dugout walls until it came out with his wad of cash. She looked at it for a moment and then put it back.

"Guess this is better than putting it in a bank," she said. "With all them closing down, you'd—"

"What are you doing?" He came around and stooped beside her.

She kneeled to the bottom of the dugout and then began knocking. "So there's the front door, the one you men see. Then there's the canals, but you already know about those."

"That's how you got in today?"

"No," she said. "I came in through here."

Her shoulder jumped and her wrist rolled and then he heard a latch go.

He leaned closer and saw, in the wood, a handle protruding. He'd never seen it before. He'd never looked that close at what was underneath. She braced her feet against the edge of the dugout and then pulled the handle, and the floor fell out. It was a trap door, like something built for a stage. He peered closer. There was nothing below but darkness.

"You got to remember, this is the second Swill," Olive said. "The first burned with the riots in 1817. So Grandma Siobhan built this dugout as a hiding spot, but it isn't much of one. If you look closely or if you've got a well-trained dog, which, of course, we've never had, you could find it. So you need something else, something even more hidden, something no one who means you harm can find, and this is that something else."

The trap door was tight for most men, but perfect for a woman. Olive dipped her foot into the dark and then stopped.

"It'll be a bit of a squeeze for you, but I think you can fit, especially since you're laying off the beer. Come on. Trust me."

She climbed down until her blonde hair disappeared into the dark.

He followed. It was tight enough that he had to leave his coat behind, but his foot found the first rung of the ladder and then the second and he let his weight pull him down as Olive coached from below.

"It's eight rungs down. Be careful."

With each step the air seemed to drop a degree, dampening with the rising smell of the sea.

"What is this?" he asked.

"You'll see. Just a couple more steps."

When he felt the bottom, he blinked a few times, trying to orient to the dark but it wasn't working. There wasn't a dribble of light through a door or window. He pulled out his lighter and thumbed the flint, illuminating Olive. She was holding a lantern and laughing.

"Light it for Christ's sake," Joshua said.

She struck a match and brought it to the wick and when the flame took and the oil burned, it stunk of fish. It took a moment for his eyes to see where he was but where he was did not make sense.

"Welcome to the Swill," Olive said.

She was right. They stood inside of a very old tavern. There were a few tables and chairs scattered before a short counter that doubled as the bar. A couple of empty beer barrels sat beside it, along with some bottles. Pewter mugs lined the shelves behind the counter and there was an American flag hanging above the shelves. Joshua counted twenty stars. Across from the counter sat a potbelly to warm the joint, alongside a fireplace and a rusted foot-stove for cooking. The walls were made of nothing but pine boards, bare of ornamentation, and the ceiling was low enough that Joshua could reach up and touch it.

"This is—"

"Amazing," she said. "Absolutely amazing. When the riots burned down the Bonny, it was a dry summer and the fire swept through the neighborhood so fast that it spared the basements and the Swill was always in the basement, even back then. The fire burned the rooms upstairs to the ground but spared the tavern. Well, I guess the old woman decided that since she had to rebuild her home, she might as well rebuild the tavern as well, so she built atop of it because it was cheaper than filling it in. It's not that strange of a choice. There's a lot of places in town like that, a whole hidden city beneath the surface."

Joshua walked around the bar, running his fingers along the bare walls, free of dust, along the tabletops and the top of the bar itself, which felt rough, worn to the bone.

"Come over here," Olive said, pointing at a door across from the bar. "It looks like a bathroom but of course they didn't have indoor plumbing. If you go through it, it leads up to a staircase that lets out of one of those metal service entrances on the sidewalk, the kind where you see restaurants dropping fruit into basements. It's the sneakiest way into the Swill, for sure. Everyone just walks right over it and never bothers to ask what's below."

He ran his fingers along the rafters. In one of them, the initials MR+JM were carved into the wood.

"Saw that too. I'm not sure who JM is," Olive said. "James Monroe? James Madison? Probably some asshole named Jim Mitchell who sold oysters. That'll remain a mystery. But I think MR is Margie Rivers, Siobhan's daughter, who, if my arithmetic is right, is our great-great-grandmother. You gonna say something, big brother?"

"I'm, I'm—"

"Dumbfounded? Flabbergasted? Stupefied?"

"Scared."

"Huh, wasn't expecting that."

"I've been looking for you everywhere and you're right under me," he paused. "Why did Grandma show you this place and not me?"

"Grandma didn't know," Olive said. "It got forgotten sometime before her. No one had been down here for a very long time before I came around."

Olive sat at a table, while Joshua stood. The lantern burned between them.

"It was before you came home, right after Grandma died. I was supposed to come home and take over. Fulfill my womanly purpose, as they say and like hell I was going to do that. It was you or no one and we couldn't find you and I wasn't sure if even we could, you'd want it. I didn't know what you were like anymore. And then, one night, I was about as low as I'd ever been and thinking of making a dumb play, something that hurt, and then, Miss Amand showed up. Hadn't seen the old witch in a year and then she just appeared inside my flop. To this day I can't say for sure if I was awake or sleeping when she came to me but she led me down to this place and told me how it had remained hidden for all of these years and said it was my very own tavern, though it's not. A tavern is where you go to be with people, but here, this is a place to be alone and sometimes I need that."

In the lamplight, Olive, with her blonde hair and white apron, looked like the ghost of barmaids past, and he imagined she wanted it that way, to evoke all that came before and all that could come after. She gave him a look with a sense of sadness, one he'd never seen before.

She reached across the table and took his hand and this gesture, the touch of his sister, broke him.

"I'm sorry," he said. "I'm sorry. I'm so sorry. I don't know what to do. I'm stuck."

"It's not a laundry list. You can run, you can go to jail, or you can turn me in. That's it. That's all you've got. I know what you're facing and I know I got you into this mess big brother."

"I knew it could go wrong."

"I didn't let you in on the whole truth. You might have thought otherwise."

"How did you think this would end with Jasper? You said you had it in the bag and I think I believed you, just a little bit. But now—"

"Oh, it's worked out for the most part, I think. He's been humiliated. People think he's a thief and he won't be Mayor. His name was what got him on the ballot. And now his name is poison."

"That was the plan?"

"I couldn't let that man become Mayor. I couldn't. He gets to represent *me*? Me. Someone he'd sooner spit on. I wanted to take that painting, that painting he had no right owning in the first place and turn it right back at him. That son of a bitch hasn't earned a goddamn thing in his life, never had a hard day and look at what he gets? He gets to step on everyone else and sometimes, sometimes when you've been stepped on enough, told you're sick, you just, you just need to throw a punch."

He lowered his eyes, didn't want her to see him crying. "I'm so sorry. I'm sorry for everything."

"Don't be," she said. "You've got a baby and a wife. No hard feelings. It's the smart move and you're smarter than most people give you credit for."

Chapter Forty-Eight

He wanted to ask how she knew he'd give her up, but he figured she'd just lie or perhaps tell him the truth, which was that she knew all her life that when it got hard he wasn't a man you could count on.

He was a man who ran.

That was his character.

He shut his eyes and remembered Olive as a girl dashing through the bar, chasing after him, just wanting to play his games, and then he thought about what his daughter would look like. He thought about all of this and knew without looking at his watch that it was almost five o'clock.

"It's time, big brother. I'll back you, whatever you decide. I owe you that much."

CHAPTER FORTY-NINE

He smoked a cigarette at the bar. He'd heard that in prison, some men stole potatoes and copper tubing to build makeshift stills in their cells, bottling lightening to keep in good with the higher-up toughs. He could see himself doing that. Even in prison, he thought, he'd still end up a barman.

"Ah, fuck."

What else was there to say? He took a drag and knew he was done talking.

After they'd come back up from the old Swill, after they'd shut the dugout hatch, but before Olive had gone down to the caverns to join Raab and Roche, he'd written three quick letters: one to Rafael handing him the Swill in exchange for five grand; one to Lily apologizing for all he'd done and saying he would not fight a divorce; and one to his daughter, to be opened in the event of his death. In that one he told her that he chose prison because she would know that he had not abandoned her or snitched on his sister, that he could not live with her thinking of him as a coward, and that he loved her very much. He gave them to Olive for safekeeping.

Chapter Forty-Nine

"You're going to be fine, big brother," she said. "It'll be a nightmare but one you'll wake up from."

Now she was gone, while up on the street, the neighborhood had quieted as the cops parked in front of the bar. He went up a few stairs and peeked through one of the basement windows. Six squad cars and a dozen police officers lingered in front of a limousine. Jasper's, he figured. It was 5:15. Olive would already be in the back of the skiff with Raab. Roche would try to extort her for more money, threatening to dump them in the Crabbe. Olive would pull a gun. Roche would agree to a lower price and then put her on a boat bound for Canada. She'd do fine up there, he thought. They also had rich people to rob.

When Joshua finished his cigarette, he filled Orla's bowl in case no one came around for a while, and then left the light on so she could find her way. He took one last look around the bar and told himself that it hadn't been a bad place to grow up and it wouldn't have been a bad place to grow old. If he ever got out, it would be Rafael's bar and maybe the old man would throw him some work if the place got busy. Otherwise, he'd have to get a job and—

Then he stopped thinking about the future. There was no point. He had to live second by second if he was going to survive, just like the War. His sergeant had said it was no good worrying about what was over the top. You'd meet it, life or death, soon enough.

So he got on with it. There were eighteen stairs altogether, eighteen stairs toward the door and he took them slow and thought of nothing but the next step. When he got to the final step, he pressed his ear to the door and listened. There were no sirens or the loading of guns as far as he could tell, just some yelling. Joshua unlocked the door, turned the knob, ready to meet life or death. He pushed.

And it pushed right back.

Chapter Forty-Nine

He pushed again but it wouldn't give. A third push let in a sliver of light, but then the door pushed back and shut out the light. It was like someone was bracing the door. He kneeled, looked out one of the small windows. The cops had their guns drawn, while Duffy shook his head. Jasper yelled from behind his Packard. Joshua looked toward the door but couldn't see what was holding it shut. A battering ram, he figured.

"I'm coming out," he said, pushing again, but the door still wouldn't give.

He went up to the second floor, hesitated, and then took the last flight up to his bedroom—his grandmother's old bedroom—because it would be harder for the cops to shoot him from that height. The room was clean, with a folded bed and a half empty closet and the lingering smell of Lily's perfume. He peeked over the windowsill hoping no one would see him but he needn't worry. They weren't looking up. All of them—the cops and Duffy and Jasper—looked straight at the Swill's front door.

There, wearing a Continental Army uniform, one that could have been stolen from George Washington's closet, stood Miss Amand. She held a musket against her shoulder and braced her back against the door.

Jasper yelled, "Get out of the way you old bitch."

But she wouldn't.

Jasper threw his hat across the street, where it bounced at Miss Amand's feet. She didn't move. Jasper turned to Duffy. "Push her out of the way and go in. Olive could be escaping."

"She's an old lady," Duffy said.

"So it shouldn't be that difficult."

With sagged shoulders Duffy started across the street, his gun holstered, because he would never dare pull on her, and then he stopped, a funny look crossing his face.

"Damn," Duffy said.

244

From out of Pirate's Alley emerged Rafael. He wore a fine black suit, black hat, and carried *Collette* by his side. The old man paused on the sidewalk, surveyed the scene, Duffy and Jasper and Miss Amand, and then came up beside her and took her hand.

"Get him out of there," Japser said.

Rafael pulled *Collette* from her scabbard and rested the saber on his shoulder.

"Mr. Castillo," Duffy said. "This isn't going to end well."

"It all ends the same," Rafael said, "be it gun or gout."

The other cops turned to one another. Joshua recognized some from school. Some pink Irish faces, along with a few Jews and Italians, and even an odd Pole. They knew Rafael and Miss Amand, knew them as they knew the way the sidewalks buckled on Bonny Lane, as they knew the smell of the Crabbe in the summer when the wind picked up. It was like pointing a gun at your grandparents.

"Detective," Japser said. "Do your duty."

But by then, there was nothing Duffy could do. Like a dog whistle, the neighborhood had been called to the Swill and they came quietly and, mostly, unarmed. Ginny Styer and her son shut their bakery, crossed the street, and stopped beside Rafael. Next came Joanna Avery and her three sons. They stood in front of Miss Amand, the boys' chests as big as the barrels of beer they brewed. They looked at the cops without any expression but resolve. Others joined them: Miguel Santos, Marjorie O'Neil, Joanie Murphy, Shauna Kelly, Jack Healey, and Henley the poet. On and on it went, familiar faces standing before familiar faces, people who'd been born in the neighborhood, or had gotten lost and found themselves marooned here, came to stand in front of the Swill. When the number passed twenty-five, Joshua gave up counting. And then, if that wasn't enough to quell the cops, Joel Vanderhock and his snot-nosed boy and the tough with the tortoiseshell glasses and a few other "reformed" sinners from the church came along and stood in the line of fire.

"Go home, Smythe," Joel said. "And don't come back."

"You sad little man," Jasper said. "I'm in charge."

And Joshua watched from up in the cheap seats. He didn't know how to feel. All of these people had stopped talking to him over the last few days; this neighborhood that had committed so many sins, sins that should never be forgiven, had now come, unasked, to protect him and Olive and the Swill itself.

But maybe it wasn't about him at all. Maybe, like Olive said, you have to throw a punch to feel human.

"Detective, your men have guns, do they not?" Jasper asked.

They did for only a moment longer before a couple of the cops holstered them and crossed the street.

"Sorry Detective," one of the cops said. "I can't."

"My parents met here," another said.

"I know," Duffy said. "I know. Lower your weapons. All of you. We're done."

"Duffy," Jasper said. "I'll see to it that you're fired."

"Beat it, Smythe," Duffy said. "Get the hell out of here if you know what's good for you."

CHAPTER FIFTY

They never caught Olive.

After Jasper lost the election, the newly installed Mayor fired the Chief and everyone forgot about "The Great Library Heist," as the papers dubbed it. None of the cops, including Duffy, lost their jobs over the botched standoff. Jasper went back to running his company. He stayed out of the papers—except when he was laying off workers—and avoided the Bonny. But he never went to jail and his business survived, just as Joshua knew it would. If Jasper still had it out for Olive, he kept it to himself.

It meant she could come home, but that didn't mean she would.

A couple of weeks after she fled town, Joshua got an unsigned postcard with a photograph of a beach. The caption read "Greetings from California." All that the card said was this: "Burned those letters. Promise I never read them."

He didn't believe her but he didn't mind either.

He had bigger problems.

The night after Olive left town, Lily gave birth to a giant baby girl, ten pounds, five ounces. Her name was Barbara.

Joshua had wanted to name her Siobhan, thought it fitting given everything he'd gone through, but Lily pointed out that no one could spell that "goddamn name."

On Barbara's first morning, Joshua went to the hospital with tulips. He walked down the antiseptic yellow corridor, wearing a suit and a face clean-shaven around the bruise on his jaw. When he got to the door, he hesitated. He hadn't spoken to Lily since she left and he only knew of Barbara's birth after Neal called to say it was done. Women changed, Joshua had been told, after childbirth. The love they had for their husbands shifted to their children and even before the birth, it wasn't clear to Joshua how much Lily loved or respected him anymore. Too much had happened to count on that. But he'd come too far to run away, so he opened the door and found Lily asleep in her hospital bed, while Barbara gazed up at the ceiling from her bassinet, her eyes blue, her hair blonde, her skin pale. He sat at the edge of the bed, looked at his daughter, and felt as frightened as that moment when he thought he was going to prison.

"You came." Lily grabbed his wrist, her eyes struggling to stay open. "Someone forgot to tell her she's half-Jewish."

"I love you."

Lily fell asleep.

After a week in the hospital, Lily went home to her parents'. Joshua visited every day, bringing toys and food, asking Lily to come home, but she said she needed time.

"This isn't forever," she told him during one of his visits. "I just need a little peace right now."

But even if things with Lily would take some time to heal, other parts of his life got a bit better. Business picked up at the Swill. Most nights the bar was filled at least three deep, and the tables were swollen with mugs and plates of food, and there was always someone at the piano leading the bar in song. The high-class jazz joints folded, one after the other, their ostentation and glamour out of place given the Depression. People came home.

Joshua sold half the business to Rafael, who took over the kitchen duties, saying Joshua couldn't "cook shit for a hog." The old man scoured Nellie's old recipes, finding deals on duck and mutton at the market, filling plates with dishes that brought tears to men's eyes, while also improving the wine list.

Joshua stayed up front, where he was comfortable. It was nice to have a partner, Joshua thought, and it was good to have the neighborhood talking to him again. No one mentioned his shunning and he didn't expect them to. And none spoke of the standoff. He once tried to bring up to Miss Amand what she'd done for him, but she waved him off.

"I have no memory of such an incident," she said. "Now, go on and fill my mug."

One afternoon, about a month after Olive left town, Molly came down the stairs carrying a suitcase. She looked as if she'd been sleeping in an alley for days. During the ruckus, he'd forgotten all about her. Molly's name never came up when he'd last seen Olive.

Joshua got out two glasses and poured two whiskeys. He'd been mostly sober since Lily left but he wasn't yet planning on making it a habit. Molly drained hers and he poured her another.

She didn't speak for a while, instead looking around the bar like it was the first time she'd been there and he guessed that was true. Olive had never brought her around.

Finally, she said, "Heard your kid looks like Olive."

"Hard to say yet but she's in there." He lit a cigarette and gave her one.

"She write you yet?"

He thought about the postcard. "No."

"Me neither but I figure she's doing fine. Cops don't seem to care about her, so she'll probably come back soon."

Joshua wasn't sure. As far as he knew, this was Olive's first trip out of town. If she were anything like him, she'd want to take her time and look around. There was a lot to the world beyond Port Kydd.

Joshua pointed at her luggage. "You living out of that?"

"Why? You offering me a place to stay?"

"If I was, would you take it?"

"Not on your life."

She opened the suitcase and reached between the mess of slips and stockings and pulled out a tin tube and laid it on the bar.

"All four paintings are in there. Figured she'd want you to have them. Imagine they're still hot so I wouldn't go selling them any time soon, if you know what's good for you."

He reached for them, but she slapped his hand.

"Fifty bucks," she said.

He gave her fifty and poured her a third drink.

"Can't believe she hasn't written once."

"I guess you always knew it wasn't forever," he said. "Olive's not much for love."

"I don't know," Molly said. "She used to talk about us leaving town and never coming back. Wanted to go down to Cuba, some place warm where no one spoke English. Always said it would be just the two of us. She was sweet that way. I figure, she left without me because she was trying to protect me."

"You really think so? Hard a girl as I've ever seen."

He didn't want to be mean but he felt bad for Molly. It was better to shatter her illusions about his sister than to have this poor kid holding onto them for years.

"Nah. She wasn't that hard. When she was scared I used to hold her under the blankets, so her face was under the covers and it was all dark and she'd run her hand through my hair and tell me how much she loved me and that after this score we'd go get ourselves a hut on the beach and swim and cook fish over fires and get old together. You didn't know that about her."

He didn't.

After Molly left, he opened the tubes and laid the paintings out on the long table. Those damn paintings, he thought. Jude Kelly. Rafael Castillo. Mary Smythe. Nellie Rivers. The Black child. The Bonny. It was there and it wasn't. It was true and it wasn't.

All of this over some paint on canvas.

No, it was more than that, he knew. There was money in it. And history. And evil. And shared, spilled blood.

The door opened and he listened to the patter of feet down the steps.

A voice he'd never heard before asked, "You open?"

"Yeah. What are you drinking?"

The End

ACKNOWLEDGEMENTS

Although Port Kydd and the Bonny are figments of my imagination, much of the detail came from research into the Lower East Side of New York City. These books were particularly helpful: *The Hone and Strong Diaries of Old Manhattan* by Louis Auchincloss; *New York Life at the Turn of the Century* by Joseph Bryan; *Gotham: A History of New York City to 1898* by Edwin G. Burrows and Mike Wallace; *Unearthing Gotham: the Archaeology of New York City* by Anne-Marie Cantwell and Dianna diZerega Wall; *Manhattan in Maps 1527-2014* by Paul Cohen; *Terrible Honesty: Mongrel Manhattan in the 1920s* by Ann Douglas; *The WPA guide to New York City* by the Federal Writers' Project; *The Bowery: A History of Grit, Graft, and Grandeur* by Eric Ferrara; *The History and Stories of the Best Bars of New York* by Jeff Klein; *Last Call* by Daniel Okrent; *Low Life* Luc Sante.

For the art and architecture of the period, I turned to *The Museum of Lost Art* by Noah Charney; *Art Forgery: The History of a Modern Obsession* by Thierry Lenain; *The Chronicle of Western Costume* by John Peacock; *Women Impressionists* by Ingrid Pfeiffer; *The Architecture of New York City* by Donald Martin

Acknowledgements

Reynolds; *Understanding Architecture: Its Elements, History, and Meaning* by Leland M. Roth; *Art: Authenticity, Restoration, Forgery* by David A. Scott; *American Artists Materials: A Guide to Stretchers, Millboards, and Stencil Marks.*

A Feathered River Across the Sky: The Passenger Pigeon's Flight to Extinction by Joel Greenberg provided context for the majesty of the passenger pigeons and their extinction.

These books helped contextualize World War I and the brutal aftermath for the surviving soldiers: *Rites of Spring: The Great War and the Birth of the Modern Age* by Modris Eksteins; *The Great War and Modern Memory* by Paul Fussell; *Fallen Soldiers: Reshaping the Memory of the World Wars* by George L. Mosse; *The First World War* by Hew Strachan; *The American Army and the First World War* by David R. Woodward.

This story is about how white communities erase their history of racial violence to maintain a system of white supremacy. In keeping with the characters' limited interactions with Black Americans—which itself is a product of segregation—I did not include Black voices in this narrative. Part of this was to hammer home the way segregation warped white historical narratives, but it's also an acknowledgement that I'm not the right person to tell those stories and there are much better novelists doing this work. For the chapters on the race riot, I found particularly helpful *The Arkansas Race Riot* by Ida B. Wells-Barnett; *Race and Reunion* by David Blight; *Black Reconstruction* by W.E.B. DuBois; *Reconstruction* by Eric Foner; *Black Wall Street* by Hannibal B. Johnson; *The Great Negro Plot* by Mat Johnson; *Trouble in Mind* by Leon Litwack; *The Burning* by Tim Madigan; *The Death of Reconstruction* by Heather Cox Richardson; *Boston Riots* by Jack Tager.

Much of the Swill's look and lore was based on "research trips" to New York and Boston bars. I'd like to thank McSorley's, The Plough and Stars, The Ear Inn, Fraunces Tavern,

Acknowledgements

The White Horse Tavern, Pete's Tavern, P.J. Clarke's, The Old Town Bar & Grill, The Bell in Hand Tavern, the Green Dragon Tavern, and Chumley's for staying open into the new century. God bless you all.

Thank you to the New York Public Library's Short-Term Research Fellowship and specifically Tal Nadan for all of your help. Not only did you provide me diaries, letters, interviews, maps, and newspaper articles, but you also let me look at letters written by Alexander Hamilton to George Washington. It was so fucking cool. Apologies for my characters robbing your library.

The University of North Carolina has not only provided me a job, but funds to help research this book, including the University Research Council Grant. Thank you to the UNC's Institute of Arts and Humanities for all of your support. The librarians at UNC answered all of my inane questions and went above and beyond to do so. Same for the librarians at the New York Historical Society and the University of Houston, where I started this book. You all do amazing, vastly underappreciated work. I hope one day that you are paid more than investment bankers.

Thank you to Mary Pardo for teaching me about 19th century female painters.

Thanks to the Weymouth Center for Arts and Humanities for providing me space and time to work on this novel.

Thank you to the folks at Leapfrog Press for your work getting this novel to print, specifically Tobias Steed, Rebecca Cuthbert, Mary Bisbee-Beek, James Shannon, and Shannon Clinton-Copeland. People like you are why independent presses will live on.

Thanks to insightful reading of Søren Palmer, who not only helped with structure and characterization, but pointed out whenever my jokes didn't land.

Acknowledgements

Thank you, Alex Parsons, forever my mentor, no matter how middle-aged we've become. You gave me the confidence to keep working on this novel and told me when I needed to keep pushing myself to do better.

Brian Wilkins was my constant confidant during this long process, who not only read this novel several times in its various, much longer forms (450 pages at one point, damn), but was the co-inventor of Rafael Castillo and Jude Kelly during the composing of a long-ago attempted screenplay. I love you, brother.

The Iselins have loved me like a brother and son for over twenty years. I am grateful for you all. My sister Laura and her family have always been a source of love. I promise the next book will not involve slightly unhinged siblings.

My son Owen arrived while I was writing this book. You're too young to read this now, little man, but my love for you is on every page. Please don't be embarrassed of all the bad words.

My mother, to whom this book is dedicated, never stopped believing that a mediocre high school student from Tujunga could do something like write a novel. You've always been my rock.

Jessica, your wit, beauty, and enduring love make me the most fortunate person I know. I love you, darling.

AUTHOR

Michael Keenan Gutierrez is the author of *The Trench Angel* and earned degrees from UCLA, the University of Massachusetts, and the University of New Hampshire. His work has been published in *The Guardian*, *The Delmarva Review*, *Contrary*, *The Collagist*, *Scarab*, *The Pisgah Review*, *Untoward*, *The Boiler*, and *Public Books*. His screenplay, *The Granite State*, was a finalist at the Austin Film Festival and he has received fellowships from The University of Houston and the New York Public Library. He lives with his wife and son in Chapel Hill where he teaches writing at the University of North Carolina.

CPSIA information can be obtained
at www.ICGtesting.com
Printed in the USA
JSHW060057250822
29633JS00002B/2